To my paren

I love you.

And I am sor

Table of Contents

<u>List of the Characters in this Book</u>

Before we start, to save you the effort of trying to keep up with all the names popping up in this book, here is their list. I am good like that. You are welcome.

In order of appearance:

Victoria Ilieva – moi, a tall woman of respectable height and countless failures

Alison – my psychotherapist

Tom – my boss

Olga (Olya) – Russian friend

Iva – my best friend

Nickolay – my son, teenager

Samantha – old boss

Dora – friend from primary school

Nina – friend

Steven – my chiropractor

Valentina – friend from primary school

Victoria – yet another friend from primary school

Ivan – first boyfriend

Moira Eden – my first Reiki client

Candice – my Reiki Master

Ivo – my brother

Vanya – my mum

Introduction

'What would you like to talk about today, Victoria?'

Alison looks at me in a way that doesn't give out much (or anything, really) and about a quarter of a smile. Or, OK, perhaps half a smile. I cannot read her face, which vaguely unsettles me, as I don't know what to expect. I am pretty good at seeing through people, but not her.

Obviously; this is why she is a shrink!

It is only our third session, so I haven't quite sussed out what is going on here.

I shuffle, nervously, in my seat. I don't like being put in the spotlight. Or asked for my opinion, if I can help it. I'd prefer to keep a low profile, thanks very much. Please don't ask me to put myself forward.

I wonder how to respond to her question. If I roll my eyes at her, that would, surely, be rude, right?

I know better than that, so I suppress the urgent need to roll my eyes to the very back of my head and sigh in exasperation.

Count to ten. One... Two...

I look around, hoping she may forget having asked me a question. The therapy room seriously looks as if taken out of a Hollywood movie with the mandatory leather couch... just it isn't a couch but an armchair. A pretty comfortable one, I must admit. Which is, of course, the whole idea: to put you at ease and make you talk.

Now, that is not something I do: talk to strangers about myself. No matter how comfortable the seat, I would prefer not to have been here in the first place.

Anyway, bar the couch, and my height (I'd bet she's never had a patient of my height before, at least not a female), everything else fits the bill. The walls are covered in boring, upper class, neutral pattern paper: one you wouldn't even notice – unless you are fishing for a welcome distraction like I am. There isn't too much furniture, either, or anything to catch your eye, like ornaments or pictures. I wonder if this may be for the same reason: to keep you focused on what you are here to do – engage in a meaningful conversation.

At least it doesn't feel clinical; that I must give her. Last time I had counselling, it was in more of a medical environment. That felt different to the warmth of Alison's private house. I am not sure how I feel about this. I feel as if I am an intruder in someone else's life. It is all different and makes me nervous: I don't like changes. Or surprises. My previous counsellor always led the conversation and asked me questions. I happily followed.

Yes, I am a good follower. This is how I was brought up: doing my absolute best not to stand out.

This therapy is different. Alison is not giving me any leads. She is the one who follows, and I am not sure I like that. Most certainly, I don't appreciate being asked to come up with topics for conversations. After all, it wasn't my idea to come here. And this seems to be too hard a work!

Eight... Nine... Breathe.

'*I* don't know!' I'd like to snap at her, 'You are the therapist, you tell me what to talk about! All I want is to get on with my life, lose the headaches and just be happy! What *I* want to talk about is stuff you won't wanna know! I feel bloated and tired, I have a million things jotted in my diary that I haven't managed to cross off for weeks... I just don't have no time for *this*! I have a deadline on Wednesday and last thing I can afford is sitting here, 'talking'!!'

Or maybe let me have a nap on your sofa instead of talking; that would do perfectly!

Now, wouldn't that be lovely. Thinking about it, I will probably need a snooze in the car after work: I can hardly go through a full day of work and commute without having a short sleep before I drive off home. That can't be good...

I move my gaze from the pretty horrendous wallpaper: staring at it is not going to help me. The woman is still expecting my answer.

'I don't really know, Alison', I smile politely. 'Perhaps we should start where we left it last time? We talked about work'.

This doesn't seem to be going the way I was hoping. Although, in all fairness, I had no particular expectations. It wasn't my idea to have counselling to start with. It was my boss who suggested it during my yearly appraisal: apparently, I seemed stressed. Me, stressed? I didn't laugh at him at the time, which took some effort (I know better than that, he is my manager and all), but, seriously, I take pride in being a tough cookie. Stressful or not, whatever life brings on, I just get on with it!

As long as I don't run out of headache tablets, as this is when I do get stressed. Without them, I'd fall apart.

Thinking about it, my annual medication review is coming up... Damn, this is a bother! Through some curse, or just sod's law, each year it is a different GP who picks the short straw to do this, so I have to explain it all over again. My headaches have had pretty much every single doctor in our surgery scratching their heads. Yes, I have heard about overdosing and rebound headaches. This doctor will, again, need to know just why I need tablets so regularly, and why on earth I have two similar drugs on repeat prescription. Oh for crying out loud, just sign off the script and have trust in me. I know what I am doing. I am not a junkie, but I do need the bloody things.

It's not like I haven't tried natural ways of getting rid of headaches, either. I've had acupuncture, homeopathy, hypnotherapy, flower therapy, reflexology – you name it. Don't want to even think how much it must have cost me over the years. And – nothing. So, give me those pills! Please.

Knowing I may not have enough tablets for the month seriously freaks me out. Just worrying about that can give me headaches! I can survive a lot. And I have. Not having my regular stash of migraine pills, though, is my biggest worry. At times (admittedly, quite rare ones), I have gone without prescription tablets for a week (or even two!), but I need the peace of mind that there is a pill in my purse should I need it.

Knowing that I have my regular dosage on me, I can conquer the world. I am a superwoman.

Anyway, I am still not sure why, but Tom (my boss) suggested it might be a good idea for me to get some counselling, and the company would pay for it. I tried not to look offended, but, seriously, how dare he! Does he mean I need help?! How rude, I am not a nutcase, I beg your pardon! And I am doing quite well, in my own humble opinion.

Not that I was a nutcase when I had my first string of counselling sessions, of course. But desperate times call for desperate measures, right, and my marriage was by that point shambles, so I needed a bit of help. I, eventually, did come through to the other end, though, and am absolutely fine. I really am!

Still, this is probably kind of a rare opportunity. Not many companies would fund therapy, during office hours as well. On the other hand, it is not like I, myself, have the money (or time, for that matter!) to shell out on expensive and, quite possibly, pointless, talking sessions, so I may as well accept the goodwill gesture. Which is why I agreed to do it. Why not – if I am getting paid for my time. Can't do much harm.

So here I am, scratching my head and wondering what the hell to talk about with Alison this time around.

'Perhaps today we can talk about you? Why do you think you get your headaches? What goes on in your life outside of work? Would you like to tell me about it?'

Would I... How long have you got?! I can talk about my life alright, it might be an amusing monologue. What is the point in that, though? Something my son said the other week pops up randomly in my head. He complained that his counselling sessions with the adolescent mental health professional were a waste of time, as all they did was chit chat. I dismissed his comment: surely, therapists know what they are doing, it is none of your business to judge! They do steer the conversations to meet the goal of each session, and he wouldn't know the 'small talk' is actively carefully led by the professional.

So why, exactly, is *this* specialist, who obviously knows what she is doing, right, asking *me* to lead the way?

Oh well. I am here anyway, the company is paying; they want to help me achieve a better work - family balance, so I may as well make the most of the bloody thing somehow.

All very well said, though, but what *do* I talk about? My life, this long and uninteresting string of trials, errors and failures? You know Bridget Jones and her diary, right? Well, *that* was fiction. My life, on the other hand, is real, and is not a pretty picture.

And, where do I start?

<u>The Tallest Girl in the World</u>

Don't get me wrong, I love my parents. But it is all their fault! Sorry, mum! I know I should either speak good things or nothing of people who have passed away... But, still, you two knew you were taller than the average people (quite a bit taller, actually, considering the size of people from your generation!), so shouldn't have mated in the first place. You would have expected your children to outgrow you, and judging by your own height-related struggles, surely wouldn't have wanted to cause the same to your children!

Tall people must not be allowed to reproduce.

I know people will hate me for this statement. Yes, it is extreme, but I have some pretty good reasons for it: my whole life story. Plus, it is a free country and I can say what I think, can't I. To an extent...

If I were a lawyer, I'd have proposed a bill preventing tall men from marrying tall women. Not that my suggestion would be legally justified (discrimination and all), but still worth a shot. This is the only way to try and reduce the damage a bit. Although, scientifically speaking, it might not, as my ex-husband's parents are both short, and he still turned out tall – but at least it wasn't their fault! That was some odd genetic mystery.

My parents, on the other hand, are 180 cm and 192 cm, so should have known better!

Producing tall children spreads the misery they have been living with, and this simply isn't fair. Not when you are a girl, anyway.

My mum didn't talk much about feelings, so didn't share many of her height worries with me. She did, however, mention a few times over the course of the years that she was the tallest girl in her school. All her life she tried to stand tall and proud, although what she really felt like was a giantess. Apparently.

Ha! She was only 180 cm! That is not much!! I wouldn't mind being her height... as opposed to my freakish two metres.

I don't remember much from my early years, but there is a conversation stuck in my memory, and it clearly proves my point: they knew what they were doing...

I must have been very young when my parents sat me down and had this weird talk with me. That I would be a tall girl and it was likely that people might not treat me nicely. The word 'bully' didn't exist in communist Bulgaria, but looking back at my past, this is what they must have meant. Back in the days, my very young brain was wondering, what were they on about?

Little did I know.

Alison is waiting for me to start our conversation. Rather patiently, I must acknowledge, although I see a bit of a surprise in her eyes: surely, she would like to dig deeper and find out where this sudden rage came from. She does seem fairly non-judgmental, which puts me at ease a bit, once I realise I'd come across quite angry. Oops.

I wonder what to say. After all, I know my parents didn't mean to do *this* to me. All they wanted was to have a happy family... the same way I did. And now that my son is starting to outgrow me, I bitterly realise I have done just the same thing that screwed up my own life: created giants. Freaks of nature.

I, too, should have known better.

At least my kids belong to another generation, one of giant boys and not so giant girls. While me... I was the tallest girl in a half-a-million city, with my staggering two-metre height. For all I know, I may well have been the tallest woman in the whole country, or in the world, even. At least it bloody felt like it! I, for one, have never met a female of my height – like, ever. I know they do exist, theoretically, but haven't seen those unicorns as yet.

#

Being a tall girl in the eighties was no fun. I don't think it is much different nowadays, either. Not to me, anyway. I do have a few girlfriends around 180 cm or just over (nowhere as tall as me, obviously, but, technically, they are classed as 'tall'): none of them has ever been particularly happy with their height. Exactly my point.

'Oh, I wish I had your height!!' some shorty will randomly exclaim every so often. Not me, thanks. I'd rather be a bit more normal. Would have probably changed my life a bit...

Back in those days, the majority of the population in my home country was below 180 cm. Anyone over that would have been regarded as pretty much a giant and, as such, attracted all sort of negative attention. It didn't help, either, that I lived in one of those countries where people didn't necessarily keep their mouths shut or mind their own business. Oh no, they just feel compelled there to express their own opinions, even if no one asked them to.

It is still like that now, a bit worse even, with freedom of speech and all privileges associated with it. During good old communism there were at least some norms of social behaviour, so humiliation was a bit more subtle... while nowadays all it takes is to switch the TV on and watch a few minutes of their reality shows. Homophobic, different-to-us phobic, anything-to-make-fun-of phobic. They'd have a field day with me, if I were to be a guest of one of those shows.

I would have hated to be a teenager there now. Which is what my children would have been if I'd stayed there. Good job I got to escape to a country with a bit more tolerance towards others. In theory, at least.

Anyway. Because of my height, there was always an expectation that I'd be the most responsible and mature amongst a group of peers. Strangers assumed I was older than my actual age, too, which wasn't much fun. Same thing happens with my son now, and the worst thing is that I catch myself having higher expectations for him. I should, really, know better!

Story of my life. Which, by the look of it, Alison finds rather interesting. Really? I wonder if that is due to her professional inclination, or just personal interest. She must have all sorts of freaks sitting in this chair, and I am sure I am just one of those.

I scroll through my unread Instagram messages to show to her what unhealthy interest men seem to have in me, for one reason only: my size. Here's the latest one that makes me want to bang my head against the wall: 'Hello hands to cm??' Learn punctuation, moron! Apparently, this user has also been trying to start video chats with me... four times. For fuck's sake. Get a life. At least his previous message was grammatically correct, though: 'How big are your hands??'

What the hell is wrong with these people? I know different things float everyone's boat, but, seriously! A few years ago I got this request from someone with an Indian name who seemed to be in the modelling industry. He offered me some serious money for taking pictures of my feet with a ruler next to them as evidence of their size. I freaked out at the idea to start with, then decided to go for it. Why not, after all no one would see my face, and it wasn't like I was going to show my boobs or anything... So I swallowed my pride and sent him those photos. Easy money, hey!

A couple of weeks later he texted to say that his company had rejected the photos.

That actually hurt. Funny to admit, but it actually did. I knew that my feet weren't as nice as a young girl's ones. I, too, used to have slim and perfect long legs. Longer than the average! They used to turn heads in the streets. They still do... Although, admittedly, two pregnancies later, that smooth olive skin is a vague memory of my single past. All I have now is purple coloured ankles, red streaks and bumps. Those three surgeries for my varicose veins didn't help my legs look better, either: the damage is permanent. And I am OK with that. After all, our scars are evidence of what we've been through in our lives. Still, being rejected didn't make me feel good about myself.

'Do you ever feel good about yourself at all?' Alison asks.

This is one damn good question. I have no answer for her and just look down at my (very large) feet.

As of that guy, at least I guess I could take comfort from the thought he probably didn't suspect I was a mum of two. I do present a certain image of myself on social media and go to extra length not to post anything about my private life. So I guess I should really be counting my blessings...

After all these years, I still suffer the damage caused by my height. I know it is all in my mind. I keep on top of the latest body confidence trends and do my best to spread positivity. #loveyourbody and all that stuff. But, actually, deep inside, I am still the same girl I was 40 (ish) years ago. The tallest girl in the world. And I am not enjoying it, not a single bit.

I remember pulling out an old school photo from my Facebook archive and showing it to my son: 'Guess which one am I?' No brainer, really: the tallest one at the back.

This is not what he said, though: 'Eek, mum, you were ugly!!'

Jeez, thanks. So much for trying to improve my self-esteem.

Truth really does hurt.

#

Coming out of Alison's office, I quickly check my phone on the way back to work. In my Messenger, there is a surprise waiting for me. An old friend from Russia seems to have dug out forgotten photos from our high school years when our classes paid each other exchange visits. I look so happy there!

Here is one where I am with Olga and my best friend, Iva. I am towering between the two of them (good 30 cm higher), for symmetry. Oh my God, my hips look ginormous! Of course they did: I was wearing men's jeans.

No wonder my self-esteem was so low. Yes, I have always had a strongly built frame, but it didn't help that there was no such thing as long enough jeans for tall women in that day and age, either. All I was able to find in the shops was men's pairs – if I was lucky. Their straight cut didn't do much for my figure, but I was grateful they fitted me. Sort of. I had to wear something, you know! Who cared if it looked good on me or not... Survival 101. Mind you, I was still wearing a 34-inch inner leg at that point, but finding even that was a struggle. Looking at those photos from the future I am in, when I can find all sorts of cuts and models to emphasise my assets, I can clearly tell the difference: men's jeans don't do female curves any favours, let alone compliment them.

I didn't even know I had curves. All I could work out was that I had wide hips, so I tried to hide them under pleated wide skirts (groan!). Which, naturally, achieved totally the opposite: made my hips look even more massive – which I didn't realise. It was fashionable and created some disguise for what I wanted to hide: this was as far as my fashion sense went in those days.

Little did I know that men actually like curves. And asses. At least some men. The bigger, the better, as long as it is well shaped and in good proportion with the figure as a whole.

Feeling hurt by my son's comment about my looks, I have been browsing through those old photos trying to find evidence that I wasn't too ugly. Well, I look kind of cute. I never actually wore makeup until I was in my early twenties, so with the arsenal I have now, any semi decent makeup artist could have turned me into a proper beauty.

Back then, I didn't know that. As far as I was concerned, I was ugly and had a huge ass.

I decide to keep this thought process to myself – to prevent any more blunt comments that may come out of my teenager's mouth. I have trouble enough with my lack of self-esteem as it is...

Oh, and what the hell was I thinking wearing my hair like this? Eek. Talking about the 80's! I, obviously, must not have liked my hair much back then. I adore it now! I don't spend much time or money on it, but I try to make an effort to look after it. It is naturally curvy, thick and supple. Some women would give anything to have hair like that: it doesn't need styling and shaping. Any hairdresser's error, typically, goes unnoticed as soon as I wash it and give it some volume by towel drying. I am lucky like that. But back in my youth it seems that I didn't care about my hair – judging by all these photos. My mum certainly didn't help me look better, either. She wouldn't have known how to do it, anyway: the only cosmetic product she ever used was lipstick. So I had my own painful journey growing out of the ugly duckling that I was.

Weird stuff, going down memory lane. How much have I changed. Panta rhei...

And the only reason I am going back to those memories is therapy. Is this really a good idea? It is going to be one painful journey.

Oh well, what have I got to lose, anyway?

<u>That Mysterious Accent. And What the Hell are Ankle Grazers??</u>

'There is something I have been meaning to ask you. I hope you don't take it the wrong way... where is your accent from?'

I do know that Alison means it in a nice way. This time, there is some gentle warmth in her eyes. I don't take offense in the question... which I suppose I could do, but no, one thing I am happy to admit is, I will never lose my accent. Not that I don't want to, just can't. Sorry, I will never be British enough!

It secretly gets me jealous hearing other Eastern European girls talk like native speakers. Romanians are particularly good at it. Lucky them! I so wish I could do that! Talking like everyone else helps you blend in. I can't exactly go unnoticed in the crowd, not with this fucking two-metre height of mine, but at least there'd be one less reason for people to notice me. If I could at least hide the fact I was foreign, that would be some help.

After twenty years living in England, I still get people guessing:

'Oh, is that a French accent that I can hear?'

'Are you Italian?'

I could easily pass for either of these: dark hair, hazel eyes, olive skin. Sometimes I amuse myself by playing along and pretending I am of some random Mediterranean nationality. I do make a good Italian woman, particularly when having an argument with my husband... or when shouting my lungs out at the kids. Like I did during that first Covid lockdown, out on a nature walk starting with a loud screaming session: 'Just! Shut! Up! And! Go!!!!'

One thing I cannot do is fake accents. I take pride in being somewhat of an intellectual, but accents have nothing to do with how clever you are. No matter how much you work at it, you either do accents or you don't. Dammit.

A bit like singing, actually. You can either do it, or not. My mum was particularly terrible at it. She just loved to sing, but was so out of tune it hurt my ears. At least that I can do; I have a good voice. Not that I did anything with it, but I do like my singing while cooking. Not so much in the shower, as it echoes, but I suppose I could do it more often. It is good for releasing the tension after a long day. Still, 'don't give up your day job', my husband jokes. Oi!

Having mentioned singing brings back school choir memories. Our music teacher always used to stand me up at the very last step on stage which made me even taller, and I stood out even more than usual – if this was at all possible. Why on earth didn't she let me be at the front – I would have blended in a bit with people behind me?? And now it makes me wonder, is this why I have fear for heights maybe? Worrying that not only I am the tallest of all, but also at the highest position, so likely to get hurt badly should I fall. Which is the same reason why my most feared gymnastics apparatus at school was the beam. Think how high a normal person would be on it. Now think how much higher that would have been for me. Yup, scary stuff.

Oh, I am one weird basket case, aren't I!

Anyway, once I've admitted where my accent comes from, instead of asking the logical question, 'Where *is* Bulgaria?' (Most really haven't the faintest idea), people proceed to inquire, are all women in my country so tall? Which is when it, frankly, starts getting on my nerves. No, actually I am the *only* giantess in Bulgaria. Or was, until I left it. Now Britain has the privilege of having landed a giantess, and, as a matter of fact, here, out of all countries, I'd expect not to get grief for the one thing I can do nothing about: my height!

Hm... it is an interesting thought process that I have: just how did I arrive at my height again, after talking about my accent and my singing?

Perhaps I should just be honest and start from where I should have: admit it to Alison. My height, somehow, created the biggest problems in my life. It gave me all those complexes I had to overcome through my teenage years and well into my twenties. It led, eventually, to low self-esteem that fucked up most of my adult life.

There. I said it! I have cracked open. Therapy obviously works.

Can I go back to the office now? Please. I have done enough of this self-analysis.

I am not ready to let this go, though... Once the kraken is unleashed, you'd have a bit of a job pushing it back into its cave! How I got to dig this deep hole for myself, I don't really know. I had lovely friends who didn't give a toss I was 30 cm taller. Neither did my teachers who loved how I excelled academically and challenged me to achieve more. Still, I don't remember being liked. All I remember from my younger years is being called all sorts, and somehow all this verbal abuse must have got to me.

People would always stare at me. Sometimes they even looked scared, as if I was a monster or something. Others picked on me just because they knew they'd get away with it, because people would always assume that it is the big one doing the abusing, not the 'normal' one...

Perhaps it would be therapeutic to bring all this out, once and for all, and be done with it? Instead of trying to chase the kraken away, like I have been doing all my life, actually let it show its head properly?

Or not. It is really very boring. This therapy is doing my head in. Just leave me to get on with my life. Please. It is a mess enough as it is, and the real reason I never wanted counselling is not money. I just don't want to dig into my own dirty laundry. I don't want to get upset – which is what eventually will happen. I have a job to go back to, and I need to be my organised and efficient self, not a red blotch of a face with watery puffy eyes. Plus, crying gives me horrendous headaches.

Aren't these 45 minutes through by now, anyway?

#

I do remember laughing about my height – once. Mum and I were walking down a busy street in the town centre. I wore trousers that were a tad on the short side. Up to my ankle, to be more precise, so yes, I know, quite bad. This is the early 80's we are talking about; not current times when you can wear trousers as short or as long as you please. We're also talking about a country where people just like getting their noses into other people's business!

Nowadays, you can get away with wearing pretty much anything. These are now called 'ankle grazers': one of those fashion mysteries for me. Just the way these are called gives me shivers! I spent my entire childhood desperately trying not to look like I'd grown out of my clothes, which is, ironically, what I was most of the time. Why on earth would I choose to dress that way on purpose?!

I remember browsing through specialist tall clothing websites once and scratching my head: why, just why, would I pay for overpriced seven eighths trousers (or three quarters length sleeves, or miniskirts for that matter), when I can get that look in the 'normal' shops, where clothes are simply too short for me?!

While scrolling through, I amused myself reading the customer reviews. Some ladies loved the rise and the fit, so OK, fair enough. I know that specialised tall retailers pay attention to the sizing measurements and their clothes fit in the right places. I get that. There were some customers, though, who made a clear choice to send the trousers back. 'Ankle grazers!' read one review. 'Never again! It just looks like you've grown out of your trousers! Which I think it's fair to say brings out PTSD type symptoms in most of us. The degradation and humiliation we went through in childhood/early adulthood will never make them a fashion choice for me!'

I chucked reading that, and related to it. Oh boy, I did!

I was just growing *so* fast that there was no point in going through the trouble of sourcing a new pair, only to realise in a few weeks that they would be too short, anyway. It made the job of my mum's tailor of making trousers for me pretty pointless, as it felt like I was always on the hunt for a new pair to fit my ever growing pins.

What I should also explain is that no shops catered for non-standard people like me. I don't think they still do, actually. The amount of time I have been raiding the shops on the lookout for a new pair of jeans! Once, I managed to find my length in the last possible shop just as I was giving up hope. That gave me the most enormous satisfaction! Needless to say, that was a men's pair. I wore it until it literally fell apart; the fabric thinned out and gave up on me.

I no longer go into the clothes shops in Bulgaria nowadays when I am back there on vacation. At least not for anything height specific. I can, of course, find shorts, skirts or t-shirts to fit me, just they look shorter on me than originally intended. A straight cut dress, for instance, I'd wear as a tunic, or a t-shirt – as a crop top: that kind of stuff. I have learnt to count my blessings that at least some things I can adapt for myself. Plus, crop trousers are rather trendy nowadays.

A couple of years ago I did, actually, decide to raise the question about tall specific clothes once in a shop. I thought it would be worth a shot; the prices in local currency worked out cheaper than what I would have paid in British pounds. After all, the country is now in the European Union and it is supposed to be all inclusive and stuff. Market economy should have helped source some unusual sizes, surely!

Anyway, all I wanted to know was if they had a top in tall size. The assistant shouted across the shop: 'No, sorry, we only do it in normal!' Jeez, that was subtle. I wish I could disappear in the ground at that point: everyone's eyes were on me.

I decided to try my luck in a little boutique as well. Who knows, perhaps small businesses might have spotted by now a window of opportunity here?? After all, there are more tall women in Bulgaria nowadays as opposed to the eighties, or the nineties. You'd think so. No, she just looked at me up and down and blurted out: 'You won't find anything in here to fit you!'

That's the standard of retail service in Bulgaria... but this is a whole new topic, and yet another reason why I'd rather stay away from their clothing shops.

Back in my younger years, I did find a solution. I have never been crafty, so could not make my own clothes, but one of my best friend's mum was a tailor. Very talented, too, which was a real blessing. As soon as I started having my own money (which wasn't until I went to uni where I got a monthly stipend for academic excellence), I became her regular client. Every month I ordered my own private tailor to make me a piece of clothing, which in those years wasn't particularly expensive or anything. Little by little, my wardrobe was starting to fill up with things that I liked and actually fitted me.

Luckily, by that time I'd stopped growing. Thanks God for that! Otherwise I would have had to start all over again if I were to outgrow everything I'd invested my hard earned cash into.

I had no solution for my feet, though. Literally no ladies' shop sold anything that would barely fit me. This is still the case now. My endless trips around the shops would inevitably turn into a search for men's shoes that looked slightly less masculine and would not have attracted that much attention towards my flippers. Not that I succeeded much – which added to my frustration. This must have been what my parents warned me about! How would people *not* ridicule me?? Any girl would look funny looking like Charles Chaplin, after all.

I recently came across some photos from the nineties where I was clearly dressed up. Or must have tried to be. Looking down at my feet, I cringe. As much as my tailor had made an effort to make something nice for me, all it took to kill the look is a brief glimpse at my shoes: chunky or not so chunky, there were glaringly obviously men's.

I am certain now that the reason why my feet look a bit weird is all those shoes that never fitted me well. Remember I had the photos of my feet rejected? Well, thinking about that, my toes were often squashed trying to fit into smaller shoes. Gents' shoes were harder, too, and their shape was not quite what I needed it to be, although I didn't really know that. I could only tell the difference in my late twenties when I got to buy my first pair of actual ladies shoes in England. By then, it was already too late; the damage was done. What other choice did I have, though? Having them made to measure wasn't really an option for me, either: small private businesses weren't allowed under communism and the state factories only catered up to size 41. My shoe size is 46. Ouch.

People regularly ask me about the size of my feet. I decided to never again tell anyone my shoe size after the first couple of times! If I did, they'd look at me with a mixture of disgust, amazement and some weird relief that their feet weren't that big. I felt isolated and hurt. I remember thinking, 'If I just didn't have toes, then I wouldn't have needed such huge shoes!'

Thank God I was smart enough to leave my toes where they were, and not self-harm in a stupid effort to make my feet smaller.

Anyway, what I started telling Alison about is that time when I had a laugh about my height with my mum. We were walking down the street, minding our own business, when I heard that boy exclaiming behind me: 'Hey, look, this girl will fall over, her trousers are *that* long!' Clearly sarcasm, as the trousers were too short for me.

I froze for a few long seconds, feeling stung. Why would he do that? I did nothing to provoke him. I didn't even know him. Why offend me?

Then, for another few long seconds, I realised that what he said was really very funny. I suddenly burst into this shrieking laughter, and my mum, also in shock, was quick to join me, until we both hysterically struggled to breathe.

What happened to that boy? I have no idea. I don't even remember. He may have got red in the face, realising what a stupid comment he'd made. Or he may have smirked and carried on. His reaction is not something that my brain has registered. That is not what left a mark in my memory. The importance of this brief episode in my life was, however, huge. This is the first time I realised that it is not about what they say to me. It is how I deal with it that was important.

#

Another late Monday morning in Alison's therapy room. It only takes me five minutes to walk from the office to her house. I am learning to try and make the most of this stolen hour. Gifted hour – I correct myself. I pace myself and take the time to look around. I used to enjoy long walks – when I had the time. In my old job, before I relocated here, life was slow, boring and peaceful. No commute either, as I worked locally. Total opposite to my life now. Oh heck, how did this happen?

It is rather amusing to watch the busy flow of people in Oxford. As long as they don't bump into me, shoulder me or hit me with their enormous rucksacks without even acknowledging it, let alone apologising.

In this crowd here I feel strangely invisible – despite my height. Which feels very comfortable.

This is the time when I don't need to rush. I don't have to clock in for 9.00 a.m. I don't need to leg it to the car, as three people are desperate for me to come home and be a referee to their quarrels, or cook them dinner. The time to and from Alison's are the few minutes I take to myself.

Yes, I do get a lunch break; I am not being exploited. Through my own choice, though, somehow my breaks are always chocka: either running around to do chores, or grabbing an aerobics class at the gym. There is no time to waste in life, you've got to seize the opportunities when they are there!

Alison lives in an old Victorian house by the canal, a few minutes' walk from the busy city centre and the even busier train station. The house smells like a museum. It might as well *be* a museum. She has obviously done pretty well for herself. Will I get to be that comfortably well off when I come to her age…? I wonder if she may be close to retirement. How would that feel? Would that be a welcome relief from no longer having to chat to all of us weirdos? Or would she prefer to buy herself more time and keep working, as she enjoys helping people and delving into their souls?

Funny, that. Who is the therapist and who is the patient?

It is a crisp day outside. I am standing by the window, looking through the transparent curtains, trying to remember what the canal looked like in the summer. It is dull and overcast today, and the trees have lost their coats. Their naked branches look desperate – for sun, warmth, and love.

Love? Where did this come from? Trees needing love? I must be losing my marbles. Yes, I have always been the writing kind, but out of all literary genres, poetry is the one I don't get. I could never understand the abstract associations and modernistic verses. Yet, somehow the trees are hoping that love will return to their lives and make them complete... until next autumn.

Alison seems hassled. Bloody BT have cocked something up, so she has been on hold for some time. Would I mind giving her another few minutes? Sure, I shrug my shoulders. I have nothing else to do here, so I can relax.

Relax?

Now, this is a thought.

Just how do I do that?

Last time, she asked me what I do for relaxation. I did, enthusiastically, jump at the opportunity to talk about something I take interest in: Reiki. This is my latest discovery and I do feel passionate about it. My headaches haven't been as bad since I started practising it. This is what prompted my interest in the first place: trying to help myself. It seems to work – to an extent. Not so much when I wind myself up arguing with Nickolay to the point when I give myself a fully blown migraine.

In case you didn't guess it, Nickolay is my son. Beautiful Slavonic name, mouthful for most English people. No one knows how to spell it, either. They just call him Nick.

Reiki makes me slow down and do nothing. By the time I manage to relax, though, my time is up and I have to jump back to what I was doing beforehand. But it is a very welcome distraction in my days and I enjoy it. It helps me deal with whatever comes my way more easily, and do it with some dignity and composedness, rather than anger and irritation.

Alison, however, is old school. Energy work does not interest her. She acknowledges my sudden interest in energy stuff, but still insists, how often do I meditate? I look at her in puzzlement, and in desperation. I manage to squeeze time in for brief Reiki sessions as and when I need it, but meditation is a different ball game. I need a serious amount of time for that, and to properly switch off. I cannot possibly try to fit that in, too, you know. There are only so many hours in the day!

It may be time to give Alison a bit of an idea about my daily routine. She got it spot on: work is not my main stressor. Not that I am stressed, of course, but you know, as a figure of speech. Well, by the time I have done my 30-mile commute to and from Oxford, my day is pretty much gone, so I guess work has got something to account for. I wish that was all, though. The kids are desperate for my attention as soon as I get through the door. My daughter chuckling: 'Dear diary, mummy has a ritual. When she comes home from work, she always needs the toilet'. Ha ha. Very funny. You would, too, after traveling for a couple of hours.

Anyway, what was I on about...? I am so easily distracted, it is beyond a joke. Although not as bad as I used to be back in Essex! That's when I first had counselling. Only because I was on maternity leave with my daughter, otherwise I wouldn't have been able to carve time out for it, and that would have stressed me out even more. I mean, make me even more useless, as, remember, I do not get stressed. But, cross my heart, I am useless. No point denying.

I requested counselling at the time because I was in postnatal depression – or at least that was the official version. The actual reason was to reassure myself there was nothing wrong with me and I had to get out of that marriage... while my husband was confident that the reason I sought help was my absentmindedness. Needless to say, I never told him how wrong he was.

The years of my marriage were the time of my life when I systematically kept making many daily mistakes. Pretty bad ones, too, and in all aspects of my existence. Funny how I no longer do that since I left my husband and took my life into my own hands.

It may also have something to do with the fact I now have a different type of man by my side, one who respects and supports me rather than picking up on me for everything I did wrong...

What kind of errors did I make? Well, some serious shit, sometimes. Like this one. I wrote a letter to my son about this when it happened. I will probably never show it to him. But it reminds me of just how bad things were then.

I may as well bring that letter to Alison, to save myself some explanation. Then we can move on to more recent topics for discussion.

#

Diesel

My dear son,

There is something I need to apologise for, but you wouldn't understand, as you were far too young. So I am writing you this letter, which, one day, you may get to read as a grown up.

You know that time we stopped at a petrol station to fill up the car and you wanted to come out and watch me? I reacted very badly. I am sorry, darling. It wasn't because you asked anything outrageous. It wasn't you, it was me. It reminded me of something that happened when you were just under two.

I was still working at that college – remember, I showed it to you once, when we were driving past? It's at the other side of the town centre, not too far from where we used to live – at least by car. Otherwise, it took me about forty-five minutes on foot. I used to walk to work when I was pregnant with you: I didn't drive then.

I never told you this, but you are the reason why I decided to learn to drive: getting around with a child on public transport is a sheer nightmare. Which partly explains what happened that time I want to tell you about...

I was in the last days of my job at the college. I had just handed my notice in, as I got offered the job where I am now. This is when we were buying our house as well: very stressful process... You know what your dad is like, always busy, and hates dealing with institutions. That's why I was the one sorting all this out: estate agents, financial advisers, solicitors, banks... My nerves were a bit shaky - no surprise why... Not as bad as they are now, but, shall we say, I had trouble concentrating at times…

Your dad didn't appreciate this. He doesn't do stress. I am not allowed to make mistakes – for any reason. Stress is therefore irrelevant: I just have to cope with it, as it is my own bloody problem.

Not that all this is any excuse for what happened that day… but putting all this in perspective may help you understand me.

So, I filled the tank up with diesel. We had a petrol car at the time. I didn't even realise I had done it: must have been on autopilot – as I often am, with so much on my plate. I didn't know much about cars. I still don't. I just drive one.

We were having dinner that evening. It was your dad's birthday – how lucky, eh! I somehow started a conversation about the car: for some reason it seemed a bit jerky… And I realised that this started since I filled it up with… diesel.

Your dad's eyes widened with horror: 'You filled it up with what???'

I stared at him for what seemed like a century. It dawned on me. You know how you sometimes use the wrong word: diesel, petrol, it is all fuel, after all. No, it wasn't a slip of the tongue this time! It was diesel. In our petrol car!

Did he flip? You honestly don't want to know...

I remember that day vividly. I always will. This is when our marriage cracked – finally and irreversibly. When my pride was not just hurt – but broken completely. When I realised that the only reason why I was still with your father was you.

Whatever you do, your life partner should be by your side to support and understand you. Does this sound to you like your dad and me? Does it?...

You can imagine the sort of an argument we had. Or, shall I say, interrogation: why the hell I did it. As if I had done it on purpose, for God's sake! Eventually, he declared he had no time to deal with this and I needed to sort it out on my own. He'd try to look into it when he had some time, but in the meantime I should use public transport. And, frankly, he didn't really care how I would cope without a car.

You know what it meant to use public transport, darling, don't you – although we lived near the town centre and were relatively well connected. Still, your nursery and my work were in totally the opposite directions. Taking you to nursery and then backing up on myself to go to work would have taken me a good hour and a half – if I was lucky. Picking you up from nursery after work and coming home would have taken me a couple of hours. I just couldn't do this. Which brings us back to the reason why I learned to drive in the first place.

I decided to prove to your dad that I was able to sort my own shit out. (Sorry for swearing so much – but, in my excuse, I won't give you this letter to read unless you are old enough.)

The college where I worked did auto courses, so I decided to ask the mechanics for advice. After all, this is what they did for living, so I knew I would be in good hands. They smiled at me widely: 'Don't worry, dear, you have no idea how many people do this, honestly! All you need to do is fill the tank up right to the top with petrol and give it a good drive. You'll be fine, love, don't worry! Chin up and foot on the pedal!'

This was such a relief! The damage I had done wasn't irreversible. My managers couldn't help but notice the state I was in. 'Listen, Victoria, go and sort out your problem. Don't worry about taking leave or anything. You just go and get it sorted.' I felt like giving my bosses the biggest hugs ever!

So off I went, took the car out on the road to the seaside. I talked to her as if she were a human: 'Come on, baby, we can do this, don't give up on me!' And she listened. The car tuned into my emotions, and mile after mile she rode more and more smoothly.

I remember that supermarket as if it was yesterday. I stopped to have a coffee and calm down my wrecked nerves. I just had to have a cigarette. You know I do when I need to relax, otherwise I don't really smoke. That sweet nicotine numbness took over my body. Not that I could feel anything, anyway, but still.

There was just one feeling growing in me: pride. I was proud of myself. I did it. On my own. On my freaking own!!! The car was going to be fine, and I didn't have to beg your father to fix it. For once in my married life, I managed to do something without relying on him. You have no idea what this meant to me. My tiny moment of independence.

That night I went home happy, relieved and proud. I, honestly, expected your dad to appreciate what I had done.

I couldn't have been more wrong. This is when he flipped out. Totally. I just didn't get it. Why on earth... What had I done that wrong? He told me to sort my shit out, as he was too busy to do it himself, and so I did. I deserved some credit.

I know what made him that mad. This is when it hit home. It wasn't the fact I put the wrong fuel into the car. Well, it was, of course, but this is not why he lost it.

The reason for him to be so angry with me was the fact I chose not to do what he told me to. I did not obey. I broke the chain.

'Why did you drive the car? I told you not to!!'

He realised he'd lost control over me. As simple as that.

That's when our marriage ended for me. When I realised that I could no longer accept to be dominated and be told what to do. There was not much I could do about his bullying, but at least I was no longer a submissive wife. From that moment on, I knew something had changed. This is when the gap between us started getting bigger and bigger.

This is when I knew that your father was the man I lived with – rather than the man I loved and respected. I could never get over that feeling of being put down.

#

Do you know, my son, what a woman needs? A man who wants her to be happy. Who accepts her the way she is and loves her for this.

When you find a girl one day, please remember what I've told you. You marry someone because you love them the way they are. Not because you want them to change into what you like them to be. This is what your father wanted from me: to change. That's what he will always want. As sad I am to admit it to you, I have no future with him.

All I want is to be happy and respected. Not bullied and scolded every time I do something your dad doesn't approve of. A man should be understanding, not domineering. Please remember this, and don't be like your father.

#

Alison puts the letter down and looks out of the window. I may have given her something to process...

Errors... I recall having a conversation with my son's parent support worker before I even considered having counselling. 'Of course you are absent minded, you have so much on your plate! Cut yourself some slack and don't put even more pressure on yourself!'

I guess this may have been what made me think of having that counselling, after all. I'd forgotten all about that. My memory conveniently wipes stuff out when I no longer need it. Although more often than not, when I still need it.

Oh dear, what was I talking about! Yes, my regular challenges. As if it is not bad enough for me to commute every day, I also have to deliver the kids to their dad every other weekend. What is the biggie, some may say:

so many separated couples have got similar contact agreements, right. Well, ours is a bit of a more colourful one: my ex lives 150 miles away – where I lived, too, for fifteen years.

So, every other Friday and Sunday, chunks of my life disappear on the road: on Friday – to deliver the kiddies, and Sunday – to collect them. I kill myself driving 100 miles to our meeting point and then all the way back, while he is only 50 miles away from the place where we exchange the children. Which, in all fairness, is all my bloody fault. This was my own stupid idea: I suggested that meeting point hoping to persuade the court to agree for me to move the children to the other end of the country during our bitter custody battle.

Being amicable comes back and bites me in the ass now: I could have offered another place to meet, so it were more equal and not so bad for me. Right?! Now, I have to do this for another ten long years! Groan.

On a long Friday evening after a full day's work, I don't go home and put my feet up with a glass of wine; I drive instead. Then on Sunday, I don't have a leisurely day after a busy week; I drive instead.

Don't even ask how the kids cope with these trips! Thank God for smartphones, tablets and in-car DVD players!

There is a silver lining, though. I remind myself my recent realisation: it is not what happens to you, but how you respond to it!

This is my main 'me' time: the long drives without the kids. Not a particularly relaxing way of enjoying my own company, but hey ho, this is as close as it gets to that magical silver lining. This is when I indulge in my life's passion, rock music. I need time to listen to music, not just for myself, but also to do my work for the rock website I write for. Which is yet another plate I spin, but it is completely voluntary and I thoroughly enjoy it.

Hours of driving – deep black hole, responsible for a huge loss of time, and, not to forget, money. High mileage comes at a cost. This is, possibly, one of the reasons for my headaches, too: the long hours spent behind a desk and then in the car. And, perhaps, worrying about money?

No wonder I appeared stressed to my boss. How does *he* get to the office? Half an hour door to door, on his bike. Me? An hour and a half on a good day. On a bad day could be anything up to three... or more.

Alison quizzes me with a serious expression: have I considered using public transport at all? I nearly laugh in her face. Why would I? It is so much more convenient to only rely on myself and my car. This way, I can jump whenever I am needed. When I get that phone call from school to say my son has broken his leg, I run to the park-and-ride, get in my car and am on my way. When I have yet another meeting with the Head of Year and the Special Education Needs coordinator, voila, I am there. I need to be self-sufficient. Also, commuting by public transport is not possible where I live; I could only do a partial commute on the bus. And it would take me just as long – or possibly longer. Plus I would have to find somewhere to leave my car before I can get onto the Oxford bus – so, all very inconvenient.

I politely dismiss Alison's suggestion. I hate being told what to do.

I have a ready answer for everything. My life is arranged as I need it to be. It is organised as I see fit. I am not re-organising it just because someone threw a random idea at me.

'Even if it takes you the same amount of time to get to work, this would be your chance to have some time to yourself, don't you think?', suggests Alison. I look at her in dismay. Time? To myself? Ha. She must be joking.

Failure One. My Career

'I am calm. I am collected. I am calm, collected and strong. I achieve what I want, when I want it. I attract the perfect job for myself. I work in a wonderful team. Everyone respects me. My bosses respect me and treat me well!!'

I take another deep breath, seal my palms together in Namaste and, slowly, get off the toilet seat. Slowly – because I have been sat there for some time, trying to compose myself and connect with my mantras. With my higher self, or whatever. And also just because it is quite low for my long figure. Unfolding myself is always a core strengthening exercise.

Ah... Thinking about that time we travelled through Europe by car and stopped at random motorway services in Belgium. Those toilet seats were my dream: I didn't have to struggle sitting or getting up, as I always do. They kept my long legs at a right angle. Bliss.

Yeah, not even the toilet is made for us, tall people. How fair is that? Let alone tables (no way you can fit your legs underneath), bath tubs (too short for long bodies), showers (too low so have to duck down to wash your hair), kitchen worktops (so low they give you a back ache) – and the list can go on and on!

Anyway. Weird how your legs, or just one of them, get numb once you have been on the loo for a bit longer than usual. Or, I mean, *much* longer. I have been wondering, is it possible to break a leg this way? It just goes so unresponsive that I am positive, I'd just collapse on the floor and, then, anything might happen when your legs feel like jelly, right? If I wasn't such a coward when it comes to injuries, I might have been tempted to try and see what happens. Just for the sake of experimenting. I am curious like that. Will my body protect itself, or will I just flop and break something?? I don't remember who I was having this conversation with, and they said, surely that wouldn't be possible, the body knows its job, but hm... my body, does it actually know what it is doing? Is that why I have had no periods for no idea how long for no obvious reason? Fuck knows. So, trust my muscles to keep my legs out of trouble – I wouldn't.

Anyway, back to my daily mantras. Keep repeating them! Note to self: do not, remember, do not, do it out loud! People think I am weird enough as it is with my Reiki stuff, so hearing me chant mantras might not really go down well in the office.

I stand out enough, anyway, through no choice of mine, being the only tall woman in the whole building. The whole company, that is. No need to show them I am weird on the inside, too. Although some of them may suspect that already, ha ha.

OK, in all fairness, I don't really do my mantras daily. I do have the best intention, I swear I do. I do mean to chant them every day. You bring on what happens to you. Law of attraction and all that... I am doing perfectly. Really, I am. And I am not a failure. Not a failure... And I believe it.

Yeah, right. Whom am I kidding? My career is a fucking joke. A woman with God knows how many degrees and foreign languages, working in a job where all you need is a couple of GCSEs. I am counting my blessings, though, remembering what kind of a manager I had back in my old job. The woman was a proper nutcase, she was, and took sick pleasure in bullying me. Funny how I didn't even realise she was doing it, until one of my office colleagues came to tell me she felt uncomfortable listening to Samantha talk to me. I laughed her comment off, before it hit me: was Sam really a bully?

Good job her own manager was ahead of the game. She saw through it all and took my side when, eventually, I plucked up the courage to ask for her help. This did make my life at work a tiny bit easier. Apparently, Samantha was known for doing this to any newcomer, and I was no exception. It was a kind of sport to her or something. What a sad person! She had no life outside of work, so that goes to show.

She did have a cat, though.

Sam wasn't too impressed when her own boss summoned her to tell her she wasn't supposed to bully me. That gave me a bit of comfort and secret satisfaction – but I still had to face the cow every day for a few more years. Plus her bullying escalated to a brand new level: she chose to make it all personal, so continued harassing me, but in a more subtle and hateful manner. She couldn't possibly let go, not being used to people defying her bullying habits.

Me, on the other hand, I did let go. I just decided not to give a fuck anymore, which she didn't fail to notice and drove her bonkers, as she realised she'd lost control over me.

Control... Why does everyone want to control me?

Or, is the actual question: why do I let people do it?

Taking the courage to stand up to Sam was a first to me: I must admit, I am quite a coward. I know I shouldn't be saying that, as any Law of Attraction coach will confirm, but, let's face it, it is true. Plus, in my excuse, I don't just sit there waiting for bad things to happen to me. I actively shunt shit out of my life. I fight that fear and work on myself. Or at least am I trying to. Which is as good as it gets.

Story of my life, bullying bosses and intricate office politics. No wonder so many people choose to work for themselves. Eventually, you either crack and lose your mental health, or become a conformist, keep your head down and mind your own business. Or both.

It has been a while since I last thought of this. I had been doing my best to suppress any painful memories. They are not good for me.

Like that horrible private meeting we had. 'If you do not improve your performance, we will have to let you go. You are making too many errors!' No one asked, *why* I made those errors, and was there anything they could do to help. No one cared. No one does, still. We are expected to be robots, but we are people. What goes on on the inside, somehow, doesn't matter. We are bodies. That word I heard the shop manager use in my first ever job in England: they needed more 'bodies'. I was mortified. Is this Auschwitz or something? I am not a body, I am a person! A professional who left a good career behind to come to your country and slave in your miserable little shop.

This is still bugging me, as much as I try to let it go. Is it rocket science that by criticising your staff and banging on about what they have done wrong, you will not get the best out of them? Is that what they teach you at your manager's courses? I have done an MBA myself, and this is not what they taught us. Get your notes out from the dusty folders with your HR handouts and remind yourself how to treat your staff! But oh, wait, you have not done an MBA, have you, or anything to teach you this. And it doesn't come to you naturally, either. If you focus on what your staff do well, that may be a bit more motivating... You can still address errors, but you just casually mention them and make recommendations. You are supposed to support people, not humiliate them. Which is why they call you managers: to manage. Not to bully.

Would you rather them work for you because they want to, or because they are afraid you may fire them? Exactly.

Quite like my failed marriage, really. Living with him not because I wanted to, but because I feared that if he were to leave me, I would not have managed on my own with two kids.

Fear. The very word that sums up my life. Funny, that, as I realised its hold on me back in my uni days, which was far too many years ago. And I still haven't learnt my life lesson.

'Fear is the worst of the sins', said the Master. I embraced the idea of getting rid of it, having projected the novel onto my own life and admitting that fear had been controlling my existence. Still, 'Master and Margarita' is a book, while my life is real. It is not so easy to get rid of that fear... Fear of being different, of not fitting in. Fear of disappointing my parents. Of taking risks. Of God knows what else. I never had the strength to stand up for myself or do what I wanted. It was all about pleasing others. And here is where I am now, trying to pick up the pieces of what cannot be put together anymore.

Is *this* why I ended up with Alison? To try and work myself out and, somehow, move forward as a new, freer, person?

Living in fear makes you scrunch yourself into that comfortable bubble of your miserable little life. Is that life, though, or just merely some kind of sad existence... Survival.

So it all stayed with me, sour memories from my old jobs. All these years on.

Compared to that, Tom is an angel, so I do count my blessings. He just has his moments every so often. But don't we all? I probably wouldn't be a perfect manager myself, with all my mood swings at certain times of the month.

Still, being late for work always makes me stick out like a sore thumb. It wasn't like I *meant* traffic to be jammed for miles! I left the house at the same time I do every morning. They know this very well. Some weeks I make it to work bang on time, every single day! But, then, other weeks it is just sod's law: whatever I do, I just cannot make it on time. Unless I get up at, like, stupid o'clock and leave at 6 in the morning or something. Which I can never ever do, even if I wanted. I do not do early mornings. Getting up at 6.30 a.m. is as bad as it gets for me – to be in the office for 9 a.m., at the mercy of the Gods of the Roads.

It is another matter if a train gets delayed, though. No one would even mention it. If you are late because of train delays, well, such is life, don't worry about it. Everyone else commutes by train. I am the black sheep in our office family, the only one who drives in.

Before I accepted their job offer, they knew where I lived and how I would be commuting. This is how they pitched it to me: we are the best thing after sliced bread, the most understanding employer. *You* tell us what time you can get in and we will work around you. Like wedding vows: I promise you the moon and the stars, forever and ever. Happily ever after. But, of course, life doesn't always work out like that.

Career... Don't know about that!

But it wasn't always like this. I was, once, someone. Twenty odd years ago. Now it is all gone. I spend three hours per day commuting. Or more. I run around at lunch to banks, post office, shops, gym, you name it – instead of taking a proper break. Just because I live in the middle of nowhere, where there is nothing but a few houses, while things need doing and I have no choice but doing them in Oxford in the only time that is mine. Plus, even if I were to live somewhere with more amenities available, I am never there, anyway: I leave the village at 7.30 a.m. and I get back at 6.30 p.m. On a good day, of course.

Now, this is the perfect career. And work-life balance.

Not.

#

'You do what??'

My mum's voice was shaking. Shit, she wasn't going to have a heart attack, was she!! There was a long pause before she responded to the news I'd just given her. It took me a while to decide to tell her, anyway, and now I wondered if I should have done it at all.

'I got myself a cleaning job in a doctor's surgery... Ehm, a health centre, like the one I told you about, the one we have at the university. Remember I explained to you that in England they don't have polyclinics? They have these health centres here, where it is just doctors and nurses. For any specialist care, they refer you to a hospital. Not like in Bulgaria where you can see any kind of specialist in the polyclinic. Yes?'

Yeah, right, I wasn't going to get around mum so easily. She wasn't stupid. My distraction technique did not work: 'Yes, I remember that, I know. But, you do... what?'

I swallowed hard. 'I clean'.

'Like, toilets and stuff??' my mum sounded desperate. I knew what was going on in her head: 'No, tell me that you meant something else, you cannot possibly be doing what I heard. I must have misunderstood you!'

I sounded apologetic, although I didn't mean to. I didn't have to explain myself! And yet, I did: 'Not just toilets... offices, as well. But they keep it so clean, anyway, it is not hard work at all.'

Mum was silent. Oh fuck, this was a huge mistake! I should not have told her! I could have lied that I'd got myself an admin temp job of some sort. Like data entry or shit.

But why would I have to lie?! What happened to 'no job is shameful, as long as you earn your living with honest work'? I was so proud to have landed this little job. Yes, it did dent my pride. I did shed a few tears. I knew that this was not what I'd hoped for. The American dream, but in England: I did believe in that for a while. With my career record back in Bulgaria, and with the Master's degree I'd just finished from one of

England's good universities, they should just snap me before I'd bat an eyelid! Yet, interview after interview, no one was interested. The money I had squirrelled away from my generous Bulgarian salary, and from my not so generous scholarship, was dwindling away slowly but steadily. No one cared that I came to England after a rigid nationwide selection, and that I was one of the lucky top ten applicants for this prestigious award. Ten out of 300! I really was someone, and getting here was such a huge deal. This scholarship and the degree I got to finish with it were a dream for so many more who didn't even get through to the first round of the selection process.

Here, no one gave a shit.

So, eventually, you have to swallow your pride and survive. Which is what I was doing. It wasn't that I enjoyed cleaning, or was proud of this, but it was, after all, a job done honestly. I was making my own hard earned cash in the only way I could... for now. I was certain that it was only temporary. I will make it one day, I will make my mum proud. Again.

Right then, it didn't sound like she was proud of me. Not one bit.

What I did not see coming, though, was her reaction. She was scared for me. Huh?

'You have to be careful, Vicky, please, do not touch anything there, who knows what sort of illnesses they may have!! Biological waste, you don't touch that, do you? And do you wear gloves? It is your health at risk, your life!' her voice became high-pitched. Fuck.

I tried to say something back in comfort, but all it did was irritate me. Oh for crying out loud, can she not support me and show some understanding?

She went on, in desperation: 'But that job agency at your university, what did you call it, job shop or something, couldn't they help you find something... *more* suitable for you? For your qualifications?'

I gave up. I was fucking cleaning, and that was all there was to it. My career was gone. Long gone. That was Bulgaria. I was someone there. Not here. I was no one now and had to start from scratch. Unless I wanted to go back home where I would still be someone. I would be highly regarded: a Master's graduate from a British university. This was as high flying as it could get, and would get me a decent job to trampoline me back into the top of my career – even higher than I was, as I was now educated in Great Britain.

But I didn't want to go back. I was trying to make a life here, in England. And I was not ashamed!

I had just failed, badly – in my mother's eyes. And I could only hope to reinstate myself one day when I proved to her that I could make it in England, too.

And yes, eventually I did that. I now have a proper job in a proper company. But I am not making the same mistake ever again. I never told my mother that my bosses were bullies with no people skills and I was not happy. As far as she was concerned, her daughter had proven herself – again. She made it in England: she worked in an office and had her own desk! And a computer. What more could you possibly want from a job?

#

Alison gives me that quizzical look again. 'Were your parents strict?'

I consider her question seriously. I am now doing my best to engage with her and be honest. As painful as it might be. This is why I am here, right?

'Yes, they were. A bit too strict, actually', I admit.

Alison nods: 'I figured that much, yes. Did you find that you had to prove yourself to them?'

Did I?? Hell yes. All the time.

I can see what she is doing. She is trying to do that 'childhood' thing, where we go back to those years and find the answers to our life's problems. The therapists' Mecca or something. This is exactly why she is going to ask me about school now.

I'd better warn her not to waste her time on this, though. There is nothing particularly interesting in my school years, really. As boring as my mum's tired tablecloth. And there certainly isn't anything a therapist might find there.

The only thing to find there is another story of failure: my non-starter academic career. Or, rather, the dream of it.

Failure Two. Academic Aspirations

Damn, I was right. I must have watched too many movies, or read too many books, so I can predict what my therapist's next move is going to be. Sure enough, Alison asks me, softly: 'Do you want to tell me about your school experience, Victoria?'

Do I? I am not sure there is much to talk about it, really. It is a period of my life that I hardly ever go back to. All I've got left from that black hole era is my friends. It is them who sometimes remind me of episodes that make me gasp: 'Really, you remember that? I don't!' My memory is not the best, it turns out. Not compared to my old classmates, anyway.

There is also the odd funny episode that no one else remembers but me – simply because I kept it to myself, for one reason or another: like the reason why Dora and I fell out. Having had a baby at the age of fourteen, she had to leave school prematurely, so by the time she went back we'd all have moved on to other places and forgot about her.

While I was a bit of a smarty, Dora wasn't. She had a good heart, and so did I. She couldn't say 'No' to men, I couldn't say 'No' to friends. I must have been a people pleaser even as young as that. So, Dora struggled with school. Each day we were given lessons to study in each subject, and had to prepare for the next class, when the teacher would randomly stand someone up and interrogate them. If you hadn't studied, you'd be in trouble. Nothing like the system in England when you can get away with not revising regularly.

Throughout my schooling, I studied hard to be prepared in case it was me who was going to be examined at the next lesson. It was a Russian roulette: no logic to the examination process as such; whatever the teacher fancied. Typically, once you had been examined, it wouldn't be your turn again for some time, but other times, the teacher would decide to trick you and catch you out unprepared on the very next lesson (bitch!). It happened to me once, in biology, so I learnt the hard way: always be prepared! I didn't want to have a fail mark that would then take ages to make up for, and I'd have to volunteer for more painful interrogations to prove my worth, until obtaining the desired higher mark to make up for my moment of irresponsibility.

So, as diligent as I was, I made Dora's life easier and helped her get through some of her lessons easily. Every couple of days she'd come round to our flat with a pen and a notebook that grew thicker and thicker by the minute, and would patiently wait for me to write up a simplified summary of the lesson to make it suitable for an idiot to understand and memorise. I didn't seem to mind that much: I had to study anyway, so may as well help a friend. I don't remember how many subjects I home schooled her for; all I remember clearly was geography being one of them.

For the records, geography wasn't my favourite subject, not by a long shot.

At some point, this whole arrangement must have become a bit of a burden for me. I'd started to wake up and realise there could have been something else I could have done with all that time I dedicated to Dora. After all, it wasn't like I was having quality time with her playing badminton or discussing a book, or whatever it is I was doing with the rest of my girlfriends. But I didn't have the guts to tell her. So I decided to just chicken out – like a coward.

One afternoon, our doorbell rang. My mother was at home (it must have been the weekend or something, as she was never there otherwise). In exasperation, I decided to hide in the toilet and asked her to cover for me by saying I wasn't home.

Now, one thing I have to say is, my mum never lied. This was something that old school communists like her simply would not do. For her to happily agree to lie for me, she must have had enough of all this, too. I know I wouldn't have liked seeing my daughter being bluntly used by her friends, so I am guessing that my mother decided that, in all fairness, enough really was enough!

What were the chances! Before trotting off back home, Dora decided she needed the toilet.

The look on her face…. And the red colour on my cheeks… Indescribable.

It is fair to say that since that moment we hardly ever talked.

She, somehow, managed to just about scrape through school eventually. Guilt ate me up: she would have done much better with my help.

This is how people manipulated me all my life: through making me feel guilty and taking advantage of me.

Or, the reality was that this is how I let people step all over me: because I was a coward.

What was I afraid of? I didn't know back then.

So yes, I do remember a thing or two from my school life, and I happily told Alison about those 'funny' moments. The rest of it is, otherwise, quite boring. Nothing like my son who is a constant cause of aggravation or worry, and likes to keep us on our toes. Not that he does it deliberately; at least not most of the time. In contrast to him, I was the perfect pupil, and nothing really happened. No one ever pulled me up on anything. No one complained about my behaviour. I never had unauthorised absences, or any kind of absences, now that I come to think of it. My best friend Iva, though, nearly got expelled from school for systematic lateness! No idea how she still has her lawyer's licence nowadays, either: she has always been late for everything. She never even got married, either, for the same reason: driving people bonkers with her unthinkable lateness for anything and everything. I love her dearly, but she is the most absent minded person I know. Way worse than me – although that may be hard to believe.

'Pots and kettles', my ex-husband would say. He knew her fairly well.

Anyway, I travelled some distance to get to school and most mornings had to change buses. All that Iva had to do was leave her flat on time and catch one bus. I was never late; she was, all the time. But I had to perform. I was not allowed to fail at anything. I was the perfect Komsomol leader.

Everyone had high expectations from me: my teachers and my mother. I couldn't possibly disappoint.

I also wore my uniform in the way that was required... with a couple of tiny exceptions.

Now, this will require some explanation. In communist times, we had to wear uniforms, and there were strict requirements on what was allowed and what wasn't. A bit like England, but also very different. Girls were allowed to wear a skirt, but not trousers. In warmer weather, we could wear something else instead. It was a bit like a button-up dress, but one that was designed with one aim only: to make you faceless, sexless, and to wipe off any personality you might have had. The closest to it would be a medical lab coat. It was very dark blue, belted, with a mandatory white sew-on collar. The white collar was of particular importance. This is where we were allowed a hint of freedom: we could add a bit of a lace to its edges if we wanted, and that'd have been acceptable. Just.

So, if you were to wear that on its own, you'd be absolutely fine and perfectly compliant (it was a dress in its own rights). If you wanted to wear trousers, however, you would have had to wear that monstrosity over them. No exceptions were allowed.

Communism wasn't that hard-core in Bulgaria: you were allowed to express your opinion on an odd occasion. Every so often, we'd try our luck and argue with our teachers that wearing a dress over trousers was gross (at least in those days; no comment about 21st century fashion when this is actually trendy). There was not much point in speaking up, though, as teachers would, inevitably, pin you down with words. Just wear the bloody thing and get on with it.

So, on the rare occasion when I'd have decided to use my brains and break away from the norm, I'd pull up that horrendous gown over my trousers, tuck it under my jumper, or roll it up around my belt to make it nearly invisible.

Did I get away with it? Of course not.

You couldn't just walk into school in the morning – oh, that would have been far too much freedom for us to cope with! You were not permitted in without a hundred and fifty three checks: what are you wearing, is your hair tied up, if it is very long – is it in a plait, is the school emblem sewed onto your garment (or have you just used safety pins, so you could take it off as soon as you left the school premises – I was particularly crafty at this!), are you wearing any makeup, God forbid, or jewellery. We didn't bother even trying with jewellery, as it would have got confiscated within the blink of an eye. I don't remember what happened if you had dared use nail varnish. I'd guess they'd have made you remove it or something. I never tried polishing my nails until I graduated from high school.

Yes, I was eighteen when I first used nail varnish. My daughter, on the other hand, was about three. Or three and a half, maybe.

Anyway, back to communism. I studied at an elite school, the kind that you could only get into with good grades. There were other elite schools, too, where no one looked at your grades: for children of communist leaders. Discipline may not have been that harsh there, but in our school, for children of mortal communists, discipline was a bit tougher. There were always two teachers guarding the door, so no one could escape. Only one entrance, too. It was impossible to sneak in wearing the wrong clothes. One of the guardians of the sacred gate was a former military personnel. An actual army colonel, or major, whatever. For all I knew, he may as well have been a General, wearing his uniform and everything! He was entrusted with the responsible job of policing a thousand odd teenagers, mostly girls, who didn't like wearing uniforms, or at least not the way them communist teachers wanted it.

Looking back, I am guessing that my fashion sense must have started to emerge around that time – even though my parents knew nothing of fashion, neither cared for any of that stuff. Girls' clothing was always too short in the legs and arms for me. It was more expensive, too, so any school shirts that my mum got me were men's. I had to wear what she found me in the shops, and whatever fitted me: as simple as that. Matching or not: she had no clue and, frankly, didn't care. I had to get on with it.

I had one more sin, which makes me shudder remembering it (I can hear fashion police alert pinging yet again): I always tried to get away with wearing white socks over my tights. That wasn't allowed, but we found it so cool! Most times, though, I had another reason, way more practical, for this: a hole or a ladder in my tights that no one bothered repairing. Or maybe it was beyond repair, but my mum had no money or time to go fishing for a new pair, so I just had to mask the embarrassment with some socks on top.

Come to think of it, it must have been very hard for her to find tights that were long enough for me. Which would, in hindsight, explain why I was hanging on to them for dear life.

Of course, I got stopped at the entrance and asked to take my socks off. Which is, naturally, when blood would rush to my face. It wasn't enough that I was recognisable from the other end of the corridor, but I was also stopped at the gate! My height wouldn't let me hide amongst the crowd and disappear from my shame, which is all I wanted on days like this.

A tall girl must do her best to keep her head down and not be noticed – at least where possible.

I must not have always felt like obeying, though. I'd sometimes try to push the boundaries even further. I would do what I was asked at the gate, but, then, secretly, pull my gown up again or put my socks back on. Did I get away with that? Sometimes, yes, which gave me a huge satisfaction: I managed to find a hole in the system and get it my way! No one would take the trouble to follow us around school – unless they specifically bumped into us. I was one of those twenty five girls, though, who were unfortunate enough to be under the wing of the harshest class teacher, a proper hard core Soviet comrade whose only mission in life was to enforce discipline amongst us all, young girls who didn't care much of communist dogmas and dared demand freedom.

Interesting correlation, that. My mother was a very disciplined person and demanded a lot from me; and so was my class teacher. I, sometimes, felt that they'd closed in on me and I had no room to escape. I had no choice but to be an exemplary pupil! Which I, sure enough, was:

I couldn't possibly disappoint my class teacher, or my parents, by deviating from the norm. That would be a big no-no.

So, anyway, I did my best to follow the rules, yet sometimes, on a rare occasion, the rebel in me would raise her head – only to be nipped in the bud. As a result, I'd come to school with the correct dress code. I did my best to do what I was trusted to do: the right thing. I didn't want the hassle of getting into trouble. This made my life easier.

My worst horror was to disappoint my parents. Particularly my mother.

Anyway, back from fashion memory lane. My parents never had to come to school other than the regularly scheduled parents' evenings. I was achieving top marks. With a few odd exceptions, which now get me chuckling, but in those days were major dramas in my little tall life.

I got a fail mark, twice even. Both times it was in physics, my most hated subject. I just wasn't cut out that way; achieving in sciences didn't come to me naturally and took a lot of hard work. I did not want to tell my mum about my embarrassment – not until I'd earned a few high marks and was awarded top grade for the term overall, so the failure no longer mattered. I did tell my dad, though, who only laughed it off in amusement. But he agreed with me: it wasn't a good idea to tell mum until I'd properly recovered the damage.

Even then, she got mad. Properly mad. Not because I hid the truth from her for months. Oh no. She got mad because I'd failed. It didn't seem to matter that I worked hard to improve and achieve top marks again. What was more important is that I failed.

I hid my tears and buried my face in my books even deeper.

They were not going to hurt me. Their words would be of wisdom and consolation, instead of criticism and humiliation. They would teach me what to do with my life and how to be brave, instead of demanding that I did things as I was told.

They wouldn't scorn me for being less than my best and would not be disappointed in me. They would always be there for me.

I still don't know if it was about my own ambition (ego, or whatever), or my mum's. Did I want to be a high functioning achiever, or was I simply afraid of parents' disapproval? Dad didn't really give a toss, so it all boiled down to my mother.

Perhaps this was my own little bubble of feeling accepted. I was, against my own will, always noticeable, towering over everyone, had nowhere to escape. That's why the best way to fit in was to mind my own business and not draw any unnecessary attention to myself.

Alison has been listening to me with apparent interest. Now, she raises an eyebrow: 'Do you think you may have been seeking your parents' constant approval and felt under pressure to be a good girl?'

It feels as if there is a tennis ball in my throat. I don't want to answer this question. I feel my eyes welling up and look away. Those trees look a bit happier today, now the sun is out.

Alison quizzes me again. Oh, not that look again. As if she is on to something...

Which, frankly, I think she is. She has hit the nail on its head. Yes, I always sought my mother's approval. I didn't bear the thought that I might possibly disappoint her. I always had to be the good girl.

Not until one day, in my early twenties, I realised I was a person. An individual, entitled to her own will, opinion, to her own mistakes and sins. Who was entitled to being loved even when she did wrong. Not simply an object of praise and excellence, but an actual imperfect mortal.

It was alright in theory. I did come to realise I'd spent my entire youth in efforts to be the perfect daughter, yet this realisation did not change me. I continued doing what I did best: be the top student in the whole year.

It took some balls to protest, and I didn't have them.

At uni, I started to wake up and realise there was more to life than being obedient. Little did I know it was very late for me to break free by that point. The desire to fit in had eaten me up on the inside and had become part of who I was. I had to learn the hard way how to earn my independence. I was well used to that cushion of familiarity, the fear of disappointing or doing the wrong thing. I had to continue being my best. I kept saying to myself, deluded, that I wasn't being oppressed. I was doing it all through choice; this was who I was.

When I broke up with my first boyfriend, I convinced myself it happened through my own choice – not because I found it too scary to go against my parents' demands. While my university friends were living their best years, I was getting ridiculed for my strict evening curfew. This was what, eventually, drove my boyfriend away from me.

I never admitted that to my friends. As far as they were concerned, it was me who decided to call it a day, as he wasn't intelligent enough for me. He was a basketball player (so, clearly, not a rocket scientist) and had only read one book: Friedrich Nietzsche's 'The Antichrist'.

I hadn't read Nietzsche myself. It was beyond me. Me – the girl who'd read stacks of books for her degree, including most of Russia's most complicated philosophical novels.

Instead of confronting my parents, I found it easier to keep my head down over the piles of books. I enjoyed that, which helped. They were my saviour and my friends. My escape from reality. The reality of a girl who hardly ever got out of the flat to play with friends. Who was never taught to ride a bike – because it was dangerous in the big city, and an unnecessary expense: we lived in the heart of a city with excellent infrastructure and regular bus routes to wherever I could have needed to go.

My late teenage years were a blur: of realising there was more to life than this, and the fear of going out to get it. That same fear.

What the fuck was I so afraid of?

Back to Alison's question about feeling the pressure of having to be a good girl, I think it all stemmed from the fear of disappointing my mother. The need for approval. And the need to fit in. Desperately and at the cost of my own self-esteem. Which became non-existent.

#

When I was in high school, I had a dream: to own a tiny little TV, to hide under my blankets after my 8 p.m. bedtime and watch whatever I fancied. There was no such thing as smart phones or tablets in the late 80's. I was never allowed to stay up late. Or go for sleepovers. Or join the rest of the class on any of the three-day school trips organised every May. I never did that. Because we could not afford it, I was told. Or just because this is how I was kept in check. It is what you choose to see and believe, as I realised later on in life. I carefully made sure I believed what I was told.

I rarely went to my school friends' parties – but that was my own choice. I was always bored there. I felt like an outsider, and, eventually, became one. I never ever got up and danced. Not because I didn't want to. Just because everyone else was up to my armpits and I felt awkward. I did try it every so often – only to regret it pretty much immediately. I remember a couple of occasions when a guy would come and invite me to dance – until I got up and he had to look up in dismay. One of them bluntly said: 'Uh, never mind, you are too tall!'

This would get my so called friends laughing out loud. They thought it was funny, and didn't see how I'd have felt. Nowadays, I'd have probably retorted: 'No, *you*, my friend, are too *small!*' Back then, though,

I had no guts to. I accepted that I was a freak of nature and just proceeded back to my seat.

I always ended up sitting in a corner, listening to the music, trying to understand the lyrics, munching on a snack and people watching. This is, probably, one of the most useful things I ever did. People watching helped me grow up. It was like reading a book, but one with real people in it. Fascinating stuff. I developed observational skills that I was already honing through my love for reading. It helped me find maturity and pluck up the courage to leave my cocoon. Not for some time, though.

I never analysed my thoughts at that age. Now I know that I found books and studying to be my safe place. Books wouldn't stare at me and laugh behind my back. They wouldn't call me a giraffe, or ostrich, or hose, Sasquatch, toothpick, Jolly Green Giant. They wouldn't talk at me in a sarcastic tone and enquire what the weather was like up there. They wouldn't ask me what was it that my parents put in my shoes that made me grow so tall. They didn't trip me up either, or laugh at their own sick prank. They wouldn't laugh and giggle at me in the street and elbow each other: 'Hey, look over there, that girl is gigantic!'

Books became my life and obsession. Which, naturally, meant that I always got the top grades. My degree in literature and linguistics became a passion that I devoted myself fully to. I knew this was what I wanted to do. I was my lecturers' favourite student, and they knew I'd succeed. I was cut out that way: to be an academic, a geek who lived in books and not in real life.

Until, one day, I realised that the career I was preparing for wasn't meant to happen, even with the best will in the world. Just because this is how the system worked in post-communist Bulgaria; it was all about whom you knew and not how capable you were.

I only found this out after five years of pure academic excellence and optimism. In my last year, I prepared a project based on my Master's dissertation, won a scholarship which would have given me a very nice wardrobe and money to do whatever I'd fancy. What I chose, instead, was to save it and go to Russia to spend a month researching at literary archives and libraries – with the idea of then doing a doctorate based on my work. I came back with a pile of photocopying and tonnes of enthusiasm. I'd met with the widow of my favourite communist dissident author; I had a fair advantage compared to all Bulgarian academics studying modern Russian literature. This was all very new and totally unexplored. I felt like I'd discovered the purpose of my life.

Which is when my sand castle collapsed. I was told by my former dissertation supervisor that, should a place become available for a doctorate, someone else was already lined up for it. Not because I wasn't good enough. Nothing personal. That protégé was simply older than me and managed to get her foot in the door years earlier. And this is how it was.

All those books and notes now gather dust in my parents' flat. If they get thrown away for recycling, no one would even notice. There is nothing I can do about it, either. That ship has sailed.

So yes, I have to admit to Alison what I have been suppressing from myself. I've always strived to be the best: because of my parents at first, and then to satisfy my own soul searching, which crashed with post-communist reality. Since then, the feeling of being a failure snowballed. It wasn't my future to be a university academic. I struggled hard to come to terms with that.

This was one of my most painful failures. Nearly as bad as the loss of love. Now, being someone who has no career as such, it hurts to think that I never managed to achieve anything in my life.

My biggest disappointment was in myself.

<u>Failure Three. Writing</u>

I am starting to look forward to my sessions with Alison. Going back in time hurts – a lot. Yet, I seem to enjoy it in some masochistic, bitter-sweet way. Time has magically built up a wall between my current self and my old self. Or maybe it isn't time. Perhaps it is geography that split my life into two: Bulgaria and England. Two nearly equal chunks of time, experiences, gains and losses. This wall numbs my pain, and, somehow, I look at my old self through glass. As if it is someone else I am analysing, dissecting her with some sick pleasure of baring old wounds.

Is this what shrinks do? I can see how this would give you a kick. Delving into people's dirty laundry. It must be quite fascinating, and probably fairly fulfilling.

I did use to take some interest in psychology and psychoanalysis when I was younger. In another life, it could have been me sitting in the therapist's chair.

To some extent I do wish it was me dissecting someone else's soul rather Alison mine.

The autumn when I started uni was one of the many winters of discontent in Bulgaria, a country that'd just come out of communist hibernation. All students across the country went on strike. I am guessing, those who weren't fussed about politics must have been partying themselves to death drunken state – while all I did, instead, was indulge in even more reading. This is when I got into Freud, Carl Jung and Erich Fromm. I felt at home with those books. I even analysed a dream that a friend of mine shared with me. I scared the living daylight out of her, and that was the closest I ever came to having a career as a shrink.

I still remember that dream Nina told me about. She was in an empty house with a staircase in the middle. She wanted to climb the stairs but was afraid to: there were rats on each step, loads of them.

Well, interpreting this was textbook easy: the house symbolised a uterus, staircase – intercourse. I wasn't sure if Freud provided an explanation of mice, but I used my imagination: their shape resembled spermatozoids; simples, really! So this was my interpretation of the dream: she wanted to have sex but was worried of getting pregnant.

Nina didn't say a word. She just shot me one of those looks that could kill. I obviously got it spot on.

Until then, I had no idea she had been sleeping with her boyfriend. Now I knew that she did. I did feel a bit of a pang of hurt when I realised this. I had a secret crush on him. He was just a bit taller than me and quite my type. I wasn't the lucky one to get him, though: she was.

Anyway, those were the days when getting laid was such a novelty! So, some days later we were mooching around the town centre. As we were walking into a shop, she asked me with that typical girlfriend's vanity: 'Can you stay behind and check my trousers please?' Meaning: check if there is any blood on them.

She wasn't one to show emotions much, so I knew this was her way of saying 'thank you' for my dream interpretation. Somehow, this made us connect on a deeper level, as she acknowledged that I knew her deepest fears. And, of course, most of all, that was her way of telling that she wasn't pregnant after all.

I never persevered with my interest in psychology, but I still enjoy the odd analysis of people and situations. So it comes as no surprise to Alison to hear that, together with reading, I had also started writing – quietly, secretly and devotedly. She smiles warmly: 'Wow, aren't you a woman of many talents!'

This gets me laughing. Me, talents? Then I briefly remember a comment made by my chiropractor, Steven, recently. I'd casually mentioned my idea to start up a Reiki practice, as a side business, once I qualified to level two. He gasped and smiled with some kind of admiration: 'Ah, and just *when* do you think you will do that?? In between your commute and your day job? Don't you have enough on your plate already?' Which made me blush.

He did, actually, mention, on a few occasions even, that he'd strongly recommend for me to cut my hours. The long commute and sitting at a desk all day were causing me too much trouble with my neck and back: possibly one of the reasons for my frequent headaches, too. Steven took some sort of amusement from my multitasking, but also seemed to take pity on me: I was killing myself, as far as he was concerned, and had to start being kinder to myself. And yes, he, too, thought I had many skills, just didn't call them talents like Alison.

'Talents, ha ha! Many failings, rather!' I retort without missing a beat. I still find it hard to hear praise. I have managed to develop thick skin over the years, having been teased, bullied and criticised: in the street, at school, at work, and, most painfully, and hard to admit, at home. One needs to find a self-preservation mechanism after all.

Now I feel I am starting to understand why my son struggles with praise. Most of the thirteen years of his life, he has been told off, threatened and punished. Not in a physical way, of course. Same as me, his damage is purely psychological. He doesn't seem to appreciate words such as 'thank you' or 'well done'.

Oh shit. History repeating itself! And I have been unable to prevent that from happening.

I add a mental note to myself to make an effort to help Nick more than I currently am. Once I have worked out my own mistakes, perhaps this will help me sort his ones, too?

I feel I can trust Alison now. She is starting to get me. When my free counselling sessions allowance runs out, I may decide to continue seeing her and cover the cost myself. I feel comfortable enough to admit out loud to her what I never have to others: that I always liked spending time by myself, instead of meeting people. It was much safer that way: there was no one to remind me I was a freak or call me names.

Alison asks more questions, and, not so reluctantly anymore, I admit that I had yet another complex to deal with in my primary school years, created by a so-called friend, Valentina. She never really listened to what I had to say, was very fast in dismissing my stories and, basically, made sure I knew just how uninteresting I was.

This time, my height had nothing to do with this, which came to validate the fact that I was, obviously, useless.

Until then, bullies teased me for my height. Valentina bullied me for something that hurt worse: for who I actually was, for what I had to say. A complex that stung worse and imprinted deeper.

I don't understand why, but for some mysterious reason, I didn't break the connection with that girl until we finished school and we all naturally took our separate ways. I kept going round to her flat to hang with her – and passively accepted being bullied. Like a moth flying into the light, I had no guts to break away from people who treated me badly.

Even now, thirty something years on, this still hurts. It reminds me just how hard I fought to prove I was someone.

Years on, my best friends from high school showed me I *was* interesting, but by then, the damage was too deep... At least I found that silver lining: I'd realised it was much easier – and safer – to express myself in writing. Which became my other saviour.

I was good at it, too. The word must have gone round, I realised many years down the line, when I reconnected with a primary school friend on Facebook. She remembered everything about our years together! Like being in the dentist's chair for a first time in year four – which I barely had any recollection of it. I would have been about eleven years old. All I remember is screaming. When I moved up to high school in year eight, what were the chances: their dentist was that same one! Oh dear! I so hoped she would not remember me. Yet, unfortunately, she did: as soon as she saw me walking through the door of her office, she seemed ready to run for her life. Heck, what had I done to have made such an impression on that woman?!

Anyway, Victoria (my old long forgotten friend) remembered much more. We mused about the fact we shared the same name, but no one ever got us two confused: I was called Vicky, while she was called Tory. She is the one who told me that, apparently, I was widely known for my writing.

For some weird reason, I have no recollection of anything good about myself. I was convinced that my existence during those early school years was marked with being dull and boring (thanks, Valentina!). Tory helped my happy memories flood back. How I entered those kids story competitions. With a gasp of surprise, I recalled a random title of something I wrote back in the days, a story called 'Communist Blood'. It was driven by something my mum shared with me: how someone gave blood to their enemy to save their life, which is as much as I remember about that masterpiece of mine. In my defence, it wasn't the ideology which interested me; it was the humanistic side of the story that touched me and triggered the writer in me to put pen to paper. Communism did produce some good writers, after all.

I also recalled some cute nationwide children's literary magazines and newspapers, where my name regularly featured with fairly decent pieces of writing (for my age). All this was stuff I'd buried somewhere deep in my memories, and I only remembered it when my friend mentioned it to me.

Wow. I was, after all, a clever cookie. Everyone expected I'd do very well in life and would probably become a famous writer.

I hardly remember any of that. Those cut out pages, together with all my writing and journalist work done over the years to come, my pride and joy, were carefully stored in a big beautiful folder made of leather – top prize I won in a short story contest at high school. This is, now, all gone. For good.

After my mum died, God knows what my dad did, but all those precious treasures of mine disappeared. I had nothing to show for a whole creative decade of my youth. All I had managed to salvage was a few magazines that I now treasure like the apple of my eye. It still gives me tingles to leaf through those old, now dull and yellow, pages: one of the most reputable literary magazines in post-communist Bulgaria.

How I got published there in the first place is still a mystery to me. I'd just thought I'd post a couple of manuscripts to the editor-in-chief and completely forgot about it. Until the day I received a letter from one of my pen pals to congratulate me on my good story.

I rushed out to the kiosks to find that magazine. My story was there, glorious and proud! I was published professionally, together with the biggest names in the country! This should have been enough to keep my self-esteem high – only, no one really knew about this, just a couple of close friends. No one really cared that much about literature.

Still, I felt proud.

For a few years, The Big Magazine kept publishing me. Until my muse dried out and I stopped supplying them with work.

#

It was sometime during my university era. A few years had passed since I'd written anything, so I thought it might have been useful to join a writing course. I saw a poster advertising a short course run by a local celebrity, some crime fiction writer who'd made it big. I didn't read that genre, so his name meant nothing for me. Still, he was clearly famous, so I trotted along to his class.

I turned up at the first class with a thick notepad and huge curiosity. I was eager to hear the secrets of becoming a writer.

'The key to successes', he proudly explained, 'is to write!'

No shit, Sherlock, I thought, and rolled my eyes. Mentally, of course; I am good at that.

'Even if you don't feel like it, or if you feel you have nothing to say that day, you still write!' continued the genius. 'Get your typewriter out and write! Whatever comes to mind. It may be nothing. It may be stupid. But you. Must. Carry. On! It is all about perseverance and self-discipline! One day you may write rubbish, next day – rubbish, the day after – rubbish... and so on. Until the day when you come up with something of value!'

I sulked in desperation. Well, clearly, I wasn't meant to be a writer, then, was I! I only used to write once every few months, or sometimes once a year. Or less often. I was, obviously, useless as a writer.

He then continued: 'And how you will know that you have made it into big literature?'

My ears pinged. The celebrity went on: 'There are three major professional magazines nowadays'. My heart stopped when he pronounced, clearly, the name of that same magazine that featured my work semi regularly. 'If you manage to get published in any one of them, you have made it! You are a professional writer!'

I looked at him, stunned, feeling stupid and proud, all at the same time.

I never went back to that class. I was a professional writer, wasn't I! I had nothing to learn from him.

#

Another random memory from my school years pops up. My geography teacher exclaimed once, having heard of my most recent success in a writing contest: 'This girl is fire!' As in passionate; pouring her heart out into everything she does. This caught me by surprise. I blushed hard. I felt humble and shy.

I felt appreciated. Something that I did not get to experience much in my life. It stayed with me all those years. I was appreciated!

#

It was years before I started to write again. I got married to my Bulgarian boyfriend who came over to England, so, with that, my inspiration dried out. Unlike most big writers, love wasn't meant to be my muse. Marriage was one of my major failures. I always wrote from my heart and infused my work with real feelings and thoughts, so getting married eventually shut me up. Shut me down as a person as well. On far too many levels.

I buried my need to express myself into a deep hole and taped it up with a thick layer of self-censorship. I could no longer put anything on paper. I didn't dare keep a diary, either, in case it got discovered. I got burnt from a previous experience with my parents and was never going to make the same mistake again. Keeping a diary could have ended my marriage within the blink of an eye, and I would have rather that didn't happen. Not yet, at least.

Not being able to write didn't bother me much for a while. I had other priorities, like surviving. Cleaning wasn't enough to live on, so when I landed a shelf stocking shop job, I had to grab it. I had a baby, which made life even more of a challenge, so, naturally, writing ended up very low in my list of priorities. Maslow's pyramid and all...

As per Karl Marx's wise quote they nailed in our brains throughout our communist youth, 'One's state of being determines their consciousness'. Mine was certainly preoccupied with making sure we had food on the table, and, more importantly, sufficient supplies of nappies. The eagerly awaited baby events at the supermarkets were the highlights of my existence: ecstatically stocking up on boxes of nappies, I was organised and highly efficient. Which included catering for the baby's fast growth and making sure I had supplies of nappies and clothes of his next size up. This did take some skills and calculations: it was also important not to overstock on the current size which he could outgrow sooner than expected, and then my rocket science would have landed flat on its face. Needless to say, that baby was taller for his age, so I knew how to shop for a tall person.

I, clearly, had a new purpose in life, and it killed any literary inspirations right in the bud.

I also took pride in my clever shopping patterns. I enjoyed working out how much I'd saved from bulk buying and using coupons.... And this was as far as my life satisfaction went. Maslow would have had a field day with me.

When reality had kicked in, there was no brain capacity for soul food.

Until, ten years into my marriage, I realised a huge chunk of me was missing. I tried to write again. I played it safe which wasn't hugely satisfying and reminded me of just why I did not become a journalist back in Bulgaria: having to do stuff just for the sake of selling it to the papers instead of following my heart. Still, my new immigrant tales made it into some local Bulgarian academic paper. I was a novelty there: an immigrant, former graduate of theirs, who had 'made' it abroad. Their pride and joy.

This wasn't enough for me. What I'd been suppressing all those years eventually started to come out. It exploded in a few scandalous short stories that I just had to write. In deep secret, as they were based on my failing marriage. I would not take any risks of being exposed, so sent my work to a couple of professional websites under a carefully chosen pseudonym.

I didn't expect to be published. But, then, why did I send those emails? I still don't know. Same as all those years ago when I sent my first pieces of work to that literary magazine. I guess I sometimes *had* to. In spiritual language, I was drawn to do it. Something made me. My inner self, my higher self, or whatever. My spirit guide, reminding me to be who I was. Or, in normal terms: it was an itch I just had to eventually scratch.

Sometimes I wonder if my life mission may be to write. But, if so, write what? And why is it that I never made it as a writer?

I deep down know the answer to this, but don't want to admit it: being scared. To write, I had to be honest and express my true thoughts and feelings. This was dangerous, and I was as risk averse as one can get. I was trying to protect my marriage for the sake of my young children. I chose the lesser of two evils: letting go of my writing needs instead of my marriage.

The stupid cow that I was.

So, fair enough, I ended up as a business professional – not really something you'd call creative. Bogged down in life's basic struggles, I managed to screw up my only possible talent. And joy.

Back to what I was talking about... Duh. Keeping on track of my own thoughts is an exhausting job!

After trying to convince myself for years that I wasn't unhappy, eventually I gave myself permission to acknowledge my own feelings and accept them by putting them on paper. In MS Word, rather. No one prints nowadays; we are doing our deed to save our planet. 'Think about the environment before you print this email', and all that. I do what I can. I recycle as much as possible, to the point that my husband called me 'a recycling maniac'. What a warm way to talk about your other half.

Having said that, apparently, he has stopped recycling altogether since I left him. So I guess that yes, to someone who hates making an effort about this, a woman like me would have been a bit over the top.

Which is yet another life skill I take pride in nowadays.

<u>Easter</u>

My work with Alison gets more serious with every session, and now that I mentioned my stories, there is something I need to tell her that is so painful I am dreading the thought of. I may well regret delving into that part of my past. I don't want to get upset again, remembering it all.

I take a deep breath and make a start. I can always change my mind and shut up, after all. Let's try and work with her, as all she wants is to help me.

So... That day started as any other. The only difference was checking an email account that I used very rarely. It was on a Bulgarian web domain, I hardly ever used it and was just about managing to keep it from being shut down. This is the email I used for sending my stories to Bulgarian literary websites, and did so for a very special reason: my husband didn't know my password. This was the time when we still shared each other's logins, banking details and so on; I guess we still trusted each other – or so we pretended.

I don't know why I checked that particular email on that day, as I had only recently done it. Perhaps, higher powers were at play. I never believed in this kind of stuff. I, kind of, do now, and it helps me make sense of my past. But I don't mention that side of me to Alison: starting to believe in the spirit world. She is medically trained and, by default, paranormal events are not favoured by professionals like her. Plus she already has her hands full trying to sort me out as it is, so I spare her my spiritual rubbish. One of the main reasons also being the fact that I still cannot quite make sense of it myself. Spirit guides, angels and so on – I am not quite sure how I feel about this yet.

Like my favourite movie character Fox Mulder, I want to believe. Or am I more of Agent Scully? Food for thought.

Anyway, it was probably my guardian angel who whispered in my ear that morning: 'Remember that email you hardly ever check? You may want to log in! Do you remember your password, love?' Of course I did. I am good with passwords and shit. If I am good at anything in 'real life', it is being organised and planning ahead. So I followed my gut instinct and there it was: a glorious email to congratulate me on a great story and providing the link to where it was published. A happy glow filled my eyes. I still had it! My writing was recognised – again, after years of self-inflicted silence!

Damn, I had no one to share this news with. Again. Still, I felt proud.

I kind of considered giving my mum a call and telling her... but I knew she might want to know what the story was about, or, God forbid, read it. It was proper "adult" material. Now, that wouldn't have made her proud one bit. It would have given her the shock of her life. So, instead, I decided to do something useful and give my inbox a bit of a tidy up.

Scrolling through countless offers of Viagra, low cost prescription meds without prescription, millions of dollars awaiting for me to claim them (seriously, how does all this crap appear on Bulgarian domains??), I noticed my dad had just sent me a message. What are the chances, I happily thought, and clicked on it. Good job I checked this email account, otherwise I wouldn't have read his message for quite some time.

Little did I know that it contained news that would change our lives forever. Something awful had happened and there was no return from there.

Now, one thing you need to know about me: I don't use words such as terrible, awful and the likes easily. So when I do, I mean them.

#

'Vicky! Vicky! Vicky!'

I woke up from my mum's persistent calling. My face was all wet with tears. I knew, instantly. *It* had happened. She was gone.

It was Easter Sunday.

Before starting her journey to the Other Side, she had stopped by to say goodbye. I wasn't by her bedside when she'd left her body, so she visited me in my dreams instead.

That day when I got the news about my story being published, dad wrote to ask me to come home. Mom had suddenly gone into a coma that she never came out of. I spent a couple of weeks with my dad and my brother (he also had to fly to Bulgaria from the other end of the world). No one knew how long she had, so, eventually, I had to make the decision to go back to my son and husband, to try and carry on with my life while awaiting the news of her departure.

I knew it would happen at Easter. I hoped I would be wrong. Well, I wasn't. Her candle burnt out exactly when I feared it would. Easter would never be the same.

But, then, it never had been a happy time for me anyway.

#

There were more than enough reasons why Easter wasn't my favourite time of the year. Now I am convinced that there was a higher power at play here. And there still, fucking, is.

Note to self: I do seem to swear a fair bit. More than I used to. Good job I don't do it in public. It gives me some sort of weird outlet. But no, Vick, seriously, drop the swearing, girl, OK! Not lady like or anything.

Note to self number two: next time I go to Bulgaria, find a witch, or priest, or both, and see if they can help me lift that curse, as I, really, have had enough. I am convinced that someone has done a rather good job at jinxing me. No fucking doubt about that. I even have some ideas as to who that might have been.

I need an exorcist. As a matter of urgency.

So, Easter. To start with, this is when I broke up with my first man. The love that, possibly, may have been the biggest one in my life. At least it is comforting to think that I had a big love.

They say your first love is for life. As long as you don't get married is what I'd say, which pretty much guarantees to screw any relationship up. If it never makes it fully into that glorious blossom, you are likely to always have those 'what if' thoughts. Which I certainly do, all these twenty something years on. And that deep pang for something you never really had. To kill it, you need closure, which I didn't have either.

That first cursed Easter marked the reluctant end of something I wasn't ready to give up on.

Then, it was, again, Easter when my new boyfriend arrived in England to join me. One of the most important steps in my life: tying my life up with his. I was certain that Easter marked a new beginning for me this time; the reunion of two souls in love. Symbolic at its best, innit. Romantic, Christian, and sweet.

I would say now that the long string of bad things happening to me was working its course already. I just didn't know it: I was over the moon. Love really is fucking blind. Pardon my French. I may have to continue swearing... every so often. I don't get many more opportunities to let the steam out, so may as well.

As far as Easter is concerned... Well, being the time when families spend the entire four days together, it is asking for trouble. At least for families like mine, when both members of this most sacred social unit tend to spend their normal weeks away from home working. Then, for four sodding days, they just don't know what to do with themselves – or each other.

I read in a book recently that marital problems didn't exist until men stopped working at sea and started pottering about at home on weekends. There! Spot on. My thoughts exactly.

When you just see each other in the evenings and the occasional weekends, things could possibly survive a bit longer; they could even blossom, I guess. Then, when you find yourselves at home together for a longer amount of time, you might also (naturally) dare want to do something you actually enjoy and have no time for normally.

In some families, taking time for yourself and doing something you like is actually tolerated even if your other half is not into it. In some couples, this is even encouraged! I even know families where, quite often, such wishes are happily granted by husbands whose sole aim is to keep their wives happy. 'Fancy' things like reading a book, meeting up with a friend for coffee, spending a couple of hours on the phone to your family – that kind of stuff. I knew women who were allowed to do all that, and much more, in their free time, without getting any grief from their other halves. They would even go away with girlfriends on a short break to Europe, or a spa weekend...

To me, that was off limits. Dreamland. God forbid I'd do anything for enjoyment: this meant I was selfish! 'Me' time – what did this even mean? And why would I possibly want to hang out with friends, anyway? That, surely, meant that my husband wasn't enough for me!

What *was* I supposed to do during our long weekends? Naturally, to spend half of it scrubbing the house, and the other half would have been divided between cooking and browsing the shops – our interpretation of a family day out. Any time left over would have had to be dedicated to spending time in front of the telly or indulging into making love. OK, whom am I kidding: I meant lying in bed and counting the minutes before it was all over and I was left alone.

The key lesson I learnt from my marriage was: 'We didn't come to this country to enjoy ourselves. We came here to suffer.'

How about that, eh?

Anyone can see why Easter wasn't the best thing for my married life. Or me. If given the choice, I would have worked all the way through it. Which is exactly what I did in the first years of my marriage, as shop work didn't allow me weekends off. Ever since I got myself an office job, though, I was cursed to spend four days every year trying to keep my husband happy.

My most memorable Easter was highlighted by him going into a strop. As one of my girlfriends used to call it, he was on his period. That one time I decided to tackle the problem differently. I was recently equipped with new knowledge and wisdom from a popular relationship book. As men were from Mars and women from Venus, I realised I'd been doing it all wrong, so decided to put things right once and for all! My husband had withdrawn himself into his man cave. Instead of the usual conversation to clear the air that was always driven by me, I took a new approach: I left him to himself. I minded my own business all four days – exactly as the book's author suggested.

I had a very peaceful long weekend and trusted my husband to have had one, too.

Until Easter Monday when it all went tits up. He could not understand why the fuck I had not asked him what was wrong or talked to him to get things right – as I normally did. I explained, proudly, all about the rubber band that men have, and how, once fully stretched, they would go back into their man cave, so women should let them be and, eventually, men would come out refreshed and calm, and everyone would be blissful and happy. Amen!

One thing I'd forgotten to include into my clever equation, though, was the fact that he didn't read books, or have respect for them, for that matter. They simply weren't on his radar. So, trying to explain to him that what I did was because of a book was a non-starter.

Life lesson learnt: reading books doesn't necessarily make you clever!

He went totally berserk. Apparently, I was as selfish as usual, and I didn't care about his feelings, so he felt ignored and hurt. It is safe to say that this was a weekend I will never forget – for all the wrong reasons. So yes, Easter tends to leave bitter memories for me.

#

Compared to that year, all my other Easters are a bit of a blur. I long ago stopped taking mental notes of what was going on. All I remember is that I just wanted that bright Christian holiday over with, so I could go to work and restore normality. Or whatever was close to normality, I didn't care. All I wanted was for that man to be out of the house at 6 a.m., for me to get Nick up, give him breakfast and kiss him goodbye at the childminder's doorstep... and for life to carry on. Until the next fucking Easter.

Strangely, holidays were never a problem for us. Probably because we hardly spent any time together then. The in-laws would have the kids and let us do what we wanted. Which was my only chance to see my friends and catch up on my social life. Oh boy, did I make the most of it!!

Amongst the whole succession of Easter failures, there is yet another one that sticks out in my tired of bullshit mind. We had just bought a house a few months before. Our savings were wiped out by the deposit, so buying a bed wasn't a particular priority. We slept on an old mattress on the floor.

That Easter Saturday, we ended up on the motorway driving to IKEA to buy a bed frame. The previous day, my husband had told me he'd had enough and was going to move out on Monday.

You'd think that any ideas of buying anything together as a family would have got cancelled, as he was planning to leave me... Well, no: we still went to IKEA. This made no sense.

Alison suggests: 'Perhaps he was only threatening? You did mention that he'd been doing that to you a lot, threatening to divorce you?'

I consider her input briefly: 'No, I don't think so... He had it all planned and told me all about it in the car – really weird, I thought. He had already found himself a cheap motel closer to work and was going to live there in the foreseeable future, until divorce papers got sorted and all that.'

Nick was fast asleep in his car seat at the back. All I remember is being shocked and feeling numb. Why would you go together as a family to buy a bed, the very essence of a happy couple, when you have actually decided to end the family?

I was hoping this was one of the millions of threats he used to make every so often. I felt scared, confused, and bizarrely hopeful – that this was all it was: an empty threat. His usual thing to keep me under control. Using my own fear.

Perhaps this is what it was. Perhaps he realised the absurdity of the situation and changed his mind. Or, most likely, he decided it would cost him too much to move out, so might as well stay where he was. I will never know what was going through his brain that time.

Another 'happy' Easter.

#

So, I mean it when I say I *knew* mum would depart from this world at Easter.

A few mornings before it happened, I put on my DAB bedside radio, as usual. What I heard was Bryan Adams with 'We're In Heaven'. This made my hair stand on end.

'Don't be stupid', I said to myself, 'This is only a romantic song and is meant for the lovers. Happy sleazy tune. Nothing to do with dying or *literally* going to heaven, OK! Mum will come out of that coma. She cannot leave us, not yet!'

As much as I kept persuading myself that this wasn't a premonition, I knew very well that it was.

Mum's candle did burn out on Easter Sunday. As if a circle had closed. All the shit going on in my life led to that Easter Sunday when the saddest thing happened.

At least that is what I thought then.

#

It turned out, the circle was nowhere near closed. It was Easter, yet again, when I left my husband after a long, expensive and painful divorce, and moved to another part of the country to live with the man who was my knight in shiny armour, the one on a white horse with a mission to save me from my miserable marriage.

Another bright new beginning. Will it end in the same way as the previous one? Only time will tell.

What I'd want to know is, why did it have to happen at Easter again? I am going to find out. As soon as I go back to Bulgaria, I will find a psychic who can tell me what is going on. Or perhaps I should look for one here, even.

I will break this spell. It is doing my head in.

#

Alison is patiently waiting for me to speak. As always. I can see slight puzzlement in her eyes but she is professional enough not to ask me the obvious: how exactly is my Easter saga related to any of what we have been talking about? Obviously, it gives her some background about my shitty marriage, but she knows me well enough by now to work out that I am going somewhere with it.

Yes, I am. It is when mum fell into a coma that my story got published. While her life was coming to an end, my writing Phoenix got reborn.

Something within me had turned a corner.

I started writing a book.

I knew I had a mission in life and it was to write about all the shit going on in my sad little life. This is what would help me survive my miserable existence.

The title spoke for itself: 'Passport to Divorce'. It was the story of a woman who wanted to escape from her marriage but didn't have the guts to do it, or the money. She was afraid that she wouldn't be able to manage on her own.

Sound familiar? Exactly.

My character came up with a plan: to write a book, make it a bestseller and fund her divorce with the money she'd make from it.

Now, that is one hell of a plan...

I never made it to the end of that book. Life got the better of me. Again. Or perhaps so did Fear. Of speaking out. Of being found out. I was just a fucking weak coward. Pussy.

I never made it in writing. It would have taken me too much out of my comfort zone.

Fear. The worst of sins. The cause of my biggest failures.

#

I thought the fact that I received news from dad on the very day when my story got published was a sign I had to continue writing.

Back then, I had no idea about signs. I just knew I had to do this. Writing gave me purpose. An outlet. My husband's response to me being away awaiting mum's death still felt sore. This was the trigger for me to write. I still shudder at the memories of him mocking me for having the time of my life while my mother was in hospital. While my hubby was working his ass off, I was having 'fun' – by catching up with relatives and extended family I hadn't seen for years... Simply because it had been over a decade since my dad, my brother and I got to be together for more than a couple of days.

That daily ritual of going to the hospital first thing hoping for some good news, only to be greeted at the door and sent back home: 'Sorry, we are still not allowed visitors in intensive care. And no, nothing new... Her systems are continuing to shut down.' Then what do you do with yourself all day until the same happens the following morning? Meeting with our relatives felt like balm to our collective wound: honouring happy memories of our mum who was slipping away from us.

I hope that from up above she will not read the book I was working on. I am sorry, mum. This would have made you turn into your grave. Please don't read it. At least not the chapter called 'The Mask' – strictly X-rated, pretty much porn. It makes me cringe thinking you might read it – so much that I don't want to publish it here! Remembering that her daughter was with a married man, while she could have anyone else, would have been painful. Let alone any references to sex: God forbid. 'Sex is not for pleasure; you only do it when you want to have children', was mum's firm opinion. I never even tried to argue with her. Lost battle. One of the many battles I chose to never fight with her. For the same fear of disappointing.

Feels like a lifetime away since I tried to write. I am still unsure whether I could have made it work.

Note to self: change my password on my Google Drive, just in case!

Anyway, I have failed in writing, and that is that. Let's move on to another one of my failures, and lift the mood a bit.

Failure Four. Learning to Ride a Bike

So, I had decided it was safest not to keep any written records during the years of my marriage. There was one exception: my diary of how I tried to learn riding a bike. I still amuse myself with it and will probably keep it for my kids to have a giggle one day. As I am no good at any sporting activities, at the time it helped me focus and keep my sanity while attempting something that was way out of my comfort zone.

I should do this more often. Perhaps this is just what I need: a diary??

So, another one of the failures in my life, only a bit of a funny one. For a change.

Part 1

Yes, at the age of forty-one I have never ridden a bike. Funny? Nope. Pathetic, actually! I know.

It would be easiest just to put the blame on my parents, for never teaching me. They never rode bicycles themselves, though, so the thought naturally never occurred to them. We lived on a very busy boulevard, so cycling has never been on the agenda: why bother?

At least I have duly cleared my own parental consciousness: we did teach our son this important life skill. My husband, rather, as I can hardly take any credit for this.

Many years ago my other half did try to teach me. Just the one time – as I was ever so quick to give up. Contrary to what people think of me, I do actually give up easily. Far too easily, in all fairness. But this has always been my thing: when facing something new, get scared, cry my eyes out, and nearly give up. Oh the drama! Then get myself together... and do it.

Learning practical skills doesn't come to me easily. You know how I learnt to drive? You don't really want to know. Honestly. All I'll say is that one car was taken to the scrap yard during the process. And I was left with a huge ugly scar for life, including a horrible skin graft, to remind me how I learnt this skill.

Now it feels like that's one of the best things I've ever taken up, as without a car my life would have been fairly difficult.

So maybe it's time to put my mind to it and learn to ride a bike!

Part 2

Preparation is at the heart of any new undertaking. When starting a project, I have to do my own research, weigh all options (will it hurt, how much, will I gain something out of it, i.e. is it really worth the hassle – you get the idea!), ask everyone I possibly know who is an authority on this matter. Then, read and process what I've read. Who knows, after familiarising myself with the theory, the bike may decide to magically move by itself, and my body may just go with it without getting hurt. Maybe it will all come naturally to me and this time next week it'll be all done and dusted.

Part 3

Thank God summer is over, as I can't possibly show my poor legs off at all. People may confuse me for a rare breed: half-human, half-leopard. This is just how bad my legs are after my first cycling lesson. There are hardly any areas left without bruises... well, not the best sight by any means.

On the bright side of things, I was ever so proud of myself. I did actually manage to ride the damn thing, yuppie! Not without falling over a few too many times – which would have been an amusing sight, as I am one taller than the average gal, but I (carefully!) made sure no one was around. Aren't I clever!

My first time wasn't as disastrous as I expected it to be. I can take pain but in reasonable amounts, so an hour of systematic inflicting pain onto myself was pretty much my limit. Ouch, those damn pedals, don't they hurt, and why do they bash me so hard?? Hasn't anyone thought of inventing soft pedals at all?

I have mastered to perfection the skill of driving into tiny little objects with accuracy one could only envy. I was told to look where I'd like to go, rather than where I was actually going. I did try that, I swear. Still, how come I kept stopping exactly at that one empty can that I tried (hard!) to avoid?? Or that tree I was desperately trying to give a miss: how on earth did it come so close to me??

No idea. But this must be something to be proud of, definitely. No one else, I am sure, can do this as perfectly as I can!

Part 4

Now I know: I must have had a stroke of what is known as beginner's luck. A few days after my first attempt, I optimistically decided to give it another go. All those purple-black bruises had just about got less sensitive to the touch, so – time to do it again.

Little did I know that unhealed bruises hurt like hell if bashed again, so minutes into my lesson I was nearly in tears. As most women, I can be a drama queen, big time. And I was. Would be difficult not to be, though, when the damn pedal breaks your vein. Or so it felt, as the pain was so sharp and constant that it got my attention for the rest of the day. Would be a bit silly to end up in hospital for such a thing...

You can't avoid drama when your private parts are on fire, either. So no sex for a while, then. A definite no-no. (Note to self: at the time of writing this diary, sex must have still been on the menu for me!)

All in all – total failure. Only positive thing was being able to take off on my own (most times). But I don't think this is enough to make me want to try again. I totally suck.

This is why I decided to start this diary. Hoping that by writing about it I will face my fears more easily and somehow make myself do it.

Anyway, right now I don't feel like trying again. Lesson number one learned: wait until your bruises heal – completely. And it would probably help to restore your hurt pride – somehow. It's all about attitude, isn't it? A 'can do' approach is more likely to get you there, rather than feeling sorry for yourself.

Which I am very good at. I am. No point denying. I worry about my shit too much. Getting hurt, that is. Yup, I do worry too much. Shall I call it a day, then??

Oh, fuck that! I am too tall to ride a bike. Or whatever. Don't care what excuse I can find, I just don't want to do it.

Hm, the height excuse is quite a good one. This is my main problem in life – being too tall, so may as well blame it for my inability to learn riding a bike!

Drama over. Amen.

Failure Five. Do You Play Basketball?

I don't bother showing my bike failure diary to Alison: not being able to ride that thing is hardly symptomatic of anything else but lack of perseverance, so I am leaving this out of my therapy. See? I am getting good at this therapy thing! But it's worth mentioning it briefly as a preamble to my next little story for her: that sports isn't really my strongest point. If only all those coaches trying to get me into Big Sport knew that, life would have been a little bit easier for us all. It would have helped my self-esteem, too. I find it rather demotivating having to persevere with something that clearly is not my cup of tea.

That same pattern in my life: doing things to please people. Instead of just saying: fuck that, I am out!

Although, I guess, rowing could possibly have been an option for me. Maybe. If I wasn't so fed up with being chased by those sports gurus to the point that I ran a mile as soon as I saw them in the street. They were easily noticeable, like me: I could see their heads above the sea of people in the high street, so would, swiftly, take another direction and avoid them point blank. Not that they gave up easily, but I made an active effort not to engage in any talks about rowing – or anything sports related. I just wanted to be left alone.

Seriously, seeing me aiming at the ring with a basketball in my hands? This was a fairly amusing sight. I am guessing people would actually pay for such entertainment: watching a tall girl (perfect height, so sought after, for God's sake!) being so inadequate. I could be a sports comedian (if that were a thing) or something – I was that bad.

Still, it was impossible to persuade the coaches that basketball wasn't my thing. The only way to make them believe that was to give in to their pestering and join their team. Bwahaha!

This is exactly when they, eventually, got the idea. Sadly, it was far too late for them: they'd already, optimistically, decided to drag me along to some sort of a tournament.

I have hardly been more humiliated in my life. Honestly. Being just over two metres tall, attracting fans' admiring looks... only to sit on the bench and pray not to be called into the game. Or, even worse, to actually *be* called in – only to quickly disappoint everyone, and I mean everyone, so badly!

My dad had this idea fixed into his head that I was born to be a basketball star. He kept arguing with me over the subject of education. I just wanted a 'proper' degree, while he insisted on me pursuing a sports one. He always reasoned, 'You can still have a degree even if you are a professional player! You won't lose your intellect! Think what a career you could have, retire young with a bucket full of money and then do whatever you want with your life! You can still read your books while travelling on the buses with the team, right?'

Needless to say, he was thrilled when, eventually, I fell victim to this sport. Until he, too, realised I was their biggest failure.

Sorry, dad.

At least there is something they remembered me by: being that tall girl who sucked at basketball. So, there is your silver lining. For all the wrong reasons.

I wonder if there could be a Guinness record for most unsuccessful basketball player?

So, this is why, when strangers in the street randomly stop me or try to get friendly with me and, looking for an opening line to have a conversation, ask me the mandatory question, 'Do you play basketball?', I just want to scream. All I can muster at times is an awkward smile. Or, if they got me in a good mood, I would walk an extra mile and laugh together with them at just how bad I was at basketball. Or volleyball, for that matter. Or handball, too. Which was the first sport I tried to practise – and I did try! I sucked badly there, too. At least I learnt one thing: how to hold the ball in a way specific this sport, which was, obviously, no good in basketball, and got my coaches tearing their hairs out in desperation, trying to knock that bad habit out of me. Well, you can't please everyone.

Now I can hold a basketball very well. Pretty professionally, I would say. I can make a good impression that I know what I am doing. Until I try to score two points. Or, God forbid, three.

Yup, I was such a spectacular failure at sports.

With one small exception, actually. When I was young and single, I got pretty good at the gym. This was where, unlike all those other damned team sports, I didn't have to run. Basketball: you got to run like a horse. Handball: you have to be prepared not only to run, but to also happily make those plunges onto the floor. Ouch, no way. I hate inflicting pain to myself if I can help it. Which includes running, jogging, or anything of the kind. Moving? Not my favourite.

The gym was different. No one wanted me to run or make a fool of myself there. I quietly minded my own business, kept gradually putting more and more rings onto the machines, until one day their resident doctor pulled me to one side and asked, 'What the hell are you doing??'

I innocently replied, 'I don't know, perhaps I could try it as a professional bodybuilder one day?'

He looked up at me in some sort of mild shock, then backed off with a proud smile: 'Oh!! OK, then, fair enough! Just mind your knees, love, as you are so tall. If you need any advice, just ask, OK, I can help'.

He was the only person I bonded with when it came to sports. Not my basketball coaches who were trying to make me a professional player, nor the head of the women's national team who desperately hoped to get me to suck a bit less. No, it was the doctor who saw another potential in me and respected the amount of hard work I put in my workouts. He didn't hit on me, either, which helped. Unlike all those walking wardrobes who kept trying to persuade me to go out for a protein shake with them after a workout. None of them was taller than my shoulder – which didn't seem to stop them. Eek.

One of them said once that he'd climb me like a tree. I looked at him in shock and, unbelievably, managed to muster a clever response: 'No, you must be this tall to ride!'

The shock on his face: priceless. Wanker.

Little did I know that tall women were such a hit amongst short men. Years down the line, a Mexican guy would say to me in a fond manner: 'I like tall girls even if they spank me!' If I had heard that in my young years, I would have probably gone into a fit. I had no idea what I was inflicting on those men by towering over them in the gym. I am guessing now that they may have felt a tiny bit intimidated. They were probably full of lust, too. Back then, I didn't know much about sex – or men's psychology as such. I just felt awkward. Then carried on stacking more weights on and made a point of pretending I didn't see how blatantly they were undressing me with their eyes.

Looking back, I can't really blame them for trying: that was the time when I had a body so lean that I would have to absolutely starve myself to death for years now if I wanted to look like that again. I had no meat on my skin, but, then, I didn't have a life either: just work and gym.

That fell flat on its face, too. The doctor was right; I shouldn't have piled all those weights on. My knees gave up. So many years later, I wish I'd followed his advice and taken it easy. I was never going to be a proper bodybuilder anyway, not with my height and body structure. I didn't know at the time that a tall frame has its limitations and knees are particularly vulnerable to injuries for tall people. But hey, at least I tried.

I haven't given up on working out completely. But I take it easy now. I discovered yoga – my haven. Together with Reiki, it helps me stay calm and collected, and face shit coming my way. Namaste.

Anyway, sports: another tick off my list of failures.

And to all those people asking me if I play basketball, I can proudly smile at and say, 'No, I don't. Do you play miniature golf... just because you are so bloody short?'

#

I do have a favourite sport, actually. It is not officially a sport, doesn't appear in the Olympics, or anywhere, but surely takes just as much skill and effort: buying and returning clothes online. It has its own rules and failure to follow them leads to defeat. This game can be very satisfying or very annoying, depending on the outcome of the relevant round that I am playing.

Buying clothes when you are so tall is a special ritual. It doesn't involve walking around the shops or anything of this sort, as you'd normally expect.

Need underwear? Go to the shops. Need socks? Go to the shops. Need jeans? No shops can help here. Same with shirts, coats, shoes, anything height specific: I can only get it online. Potentially.

Thinking of my youth spent in men's jeans and shoes, I shouldn't really be complaining! There was no choice for me when I was younger and lived in Bulgaria, so compared to those times, anything is an improvement. The Internet is my heaven! I can find anything there! And all of it is, theoretically, my size. Until I receive those trousers which are supposed to be long enough for me (yes, I do make sure I check that inner leg is 38", all good)... but, in reality, they come up to my ankles. Or size 18 turns out to be far too tight on my hips. Oi, don't give me that shocked look! This waist is actually fine for my height, and no, I am not obese, in case you are wondering... More height needs more width to carry it – simple!

Which reminds me how my life insurance application was rejected by a very well-known company a few years ago... because of my dress size. Now, I am not one to make a fuss, but that got to me, properly. Who are they to say what my size should be?! I got on the phone to the broker and gave them some serious earache for it. I offered to send them photos of me wearing skin tight clothing. How dare they judge and call me obese? Not that I am skinny, I know, that baby fat is not going anywhere, but I aren't that fat, either!

I was livid.

The brokers submitted an appeal, and a couple of weeks later I received an actual letter of apology from the underwriters. On proper headed paper and everything. Apparently, they hadn't taken into consideration the fact I was so tall, and now that they did, they realised that my waist size (and dress, for that matter) was actually fairly normal.

Fancy that!

It gave me some satisfaction to say: 'Thanks but no, thanks'. I managed to prove my point – for once. Being tall doesn't equal second hand quality.

Had they offered me a discount or something, I probably would have managed to swallow my pride... but they didn't. Just because they'd apologised, they didn't expect to have me crawling back on my knees, did they. I, too, have my own pride.

Anyway, back to my point about buying clothes online. I grew up in a reality where my only opportunity to clothe myself was my friend's clever mum who made everything I wanted. Being a tall girl is still no joy back in Bulgaria. I feel sorry for any tall girls who still live there! I guess I am lucky, really, to live in a country where I am able to indulge in this particular 'sport'.

It takes special skills. First, you have to hone this sharp eye for spotting the opportunity – without getting yourself into a massive debt in the process. I am nothing like that famous shopaholic from my favourite book series! I, for one, try to actively be good and ignore all promotional emails. I have learnt this the hard way, trust me: after counting about eight pairs of flat black shoes in my cupboard... which all look surprisingly similar. But, hey, this pair was from a 50 per cent sale, and that one was on a Buy One Get One Free offer, so I couldn't not have it, as the special offer would have been pointless. And that one – well, the sole is slightly better quality than this one... And these shoes... Well, I had simply forgotten I had something similar and got them because it only cost me a tenner. You cannot say 'no' to a cheap pair of shoes, can you. Exactly. Plus, this is a clever investment. Next time I need a pair like this, the cheapest I'd be able to get it would be about 30 quid, plus postage. So grab it when you can, girl.

And the list continues. My mum would have gone into a shock if she were to look down on me from heaven: 'For goodness sakes, just how many pairs of shoes do you need, Vicky??'

There is no such thing as too many shoes, mum! Not when your size is eleven, anyway! And, the beauty of it is, they are all female shoes, pretty and feminine. Nothing like the shoes the teenage version of me had, after losing the will to live trying to find something that wouldn't look too horrendous with a skirt.

Which is, actually, the very reason I grew up looking like a tomboy. No point in getting myself girly dresses and skirts if all I could pair them with was... bulky men's shoes. Unless you go all grunge and punk – which I wasn't. I did listen to heavy metal, but I didn't adopt that clothing style, thanks very much.

I am guessing, this is why I can never have enough dresses nowadays. Funnily, my former mother-in-law used to insist that was exactly what I should be wearing instead of jeans and shorts. I was always in favour of practicality, and femininity was never on my radar. After all, her son fell in love with me when I was still in my sports clothing era, and I never felt the need to dress up for him.

Having said that, I, generally, never had to make an effort for men to notice me – for an obvious reason.

I only discovered my feminine side in my early forties. Better late than never! Who knew dresses looked so good on my body... Although, thinking about it, if I did know this when I was younger, I would have definitely stayed away from them: I did everything I could to not stand out in the crowd, and wearing something sexy would have been a definite no-no to me.

I did have a brief phase in the 90's when I used to go out wearing shiny full length leggings. I felt as if I stroke the lottery finding a pair long enough, so was pleased to be properly fashionable for once. I quickly decided against it, though: I was, literally, turning heads in the streets and that made me feel awfully uncomfortable.

I also get asked a lot, do I wear heels. Why would I? I am 6'5 ½, hardly need heels to make me taller, do I. Which is, technically speaking, the whole point. Although, admittedly, wearing even small heels does improve your posture, but, still, standing even taller is not something I would have voluntarily chosen. Bit of a double edged sword, so no, thanks.

So, anyway, watching those offers in my emails go past is a seriously hard thing to do. A few years ago I had actually unsubscribed from any marketing emails, as I found it hard to resist the temptation and my bank account was getting drained faster than usual. Being on maternity leave meant I had plenty of time to look at those emails and not enough money to make a living on that joke of statutory pay, so any bargains were out of reach to me for some time. Now that kids are at school and money is not that tight, I allow myself to open those emails when there is something that I need. Like, come on, if you need sandals, you need sandals, right!

To practise this sport, you keep a watch constantly. When the target has been spotted (I have managed to find something I need and can afford) – bam! I feel like I have won the lottery!

Waiting for delivery is as close as it gets to preparing for a marathon, or any important sport, just not physically. Mentally, it takes some patience and strength to wait until the bloody thing arrives. It also takes some careful calculation: how close am I to pay day (i.e. how much of an overdraft I have got myself into), how much closer to pay day will I be when the money has actually been taken off my account, and, stage three: how long until I get my refund. Some months, it feels like I have made a saving, even: getting my money back when I have gone badly overdrawn is so satisfying! Aren't I clever?

If this is no sport, what is? No way is this less intellectual than chess! Plus, when you receive that long awaited parcel: oh the adrenaline rush!

Then – the disappointment. More times than not, the whole order goes back.

There was a phase when one of my favourite clothing brands started getting their sizing wrong – very wrong, but I kept buying from them simply because I needed new jeans and there was nowhere for me to get them. In my slightly slimmer years, I wore their size 16, and 18 was huge.

Nowadays, when 18 is my comfortable size, it can also be huge, still. Makes no sense, I know. So, I decided to be clever by ordering both sizes, confident that one or the other would fit me.

Nope, they both went back. I must be size 17. Or 16.5. Neither of which exists. Damn.

So, here is phase two of this sport. Posting the stuff back, waiting for your money, sometimes forever, but eventually it lands back into your bank account.

Important stage in the process is to keep on top of it. Remember what you have sent back, and keep an eye on your PayPal or bank account. If you don't, there will always be some sneaky bugger who will try to get away with not paying. Like that website that made some lovely tall clothes and took about a month to post the bloody thing off – simply because they hardly got any customers and, apparently, made them to order. Don't ask me how long it then took me to chase my money back. At least I live in England and not in pirate Bulgaria. If I have to get my bank involved, I will, and eventually I get that hard earned cash back. Which you cannot fault. Nothing is perfect, so as long as things end well, all is good.

Until the next round. Oh, Long Tall Sally have got their BOGOF on sales items! Quick! And fingers crossed.

So, at least in this sport I am absolutely brilliant! As exhausting and, frankly, frustrating that it may be.

Messages from Strangers, Or How Not To Talk with a Tall Girl

It is time to let Alison into the proper misery of being tall.

Something weird happens when people meet a tall person. As if a switch flips inside them: they, compulsively, *have* to ask the same mandatory questions. Do I play basketball? How about volleyball? Were my parents tall? Just how tall am I, exactly? How big are my feet, in centimetres, preferably? What is my shoe size? Do I have trouble finding men? Would I date a shorter man? And so on.

With good intentions, bad intentions, sarcasm, no sarcasm, they just all have to fucking make a comment. If not asking a question, they would, surely, must at least make it clear that they've noticed that I am tall.

How observant.

And? Your point being? You seriously don't think I am aware of the fact I am tall? I, too, as a matter of fact, acknowledge that you are short, or fat, or ugly, or your hair needs another hairdresser – and the list goes on. But I don't feel obliged to state the obvious. I think it is rude, and make sure I behave appropriately.

Just because I am tall, people feel obliged to talk to me about it. How is that OK?

Would I laugh in someone's face: 'Oh crikey, you are a shorty, aren't you?' No, I would mind my own business.

Exactly.

Being tall is different, though. I never understood why. Somehow, people feel they just ought to look at me with wide eyes and exclaim: 'Wow, you're tall!' No shit, Sherlock! I didn't know that, surely? Others see this is as a friendly conversation starter. What makes them think that I want to talk to them though?

Over the course of my life, I have heard it all...

At least my family was good about it – unlike the granddad of one of my tall Facebook friends who told her every time he saw her he said that she could have parts of her arm and leg bones removed to make her 'normal' size! I shudder at the very thought. Her own grandfather, Jeez! He started when she was about fifteen, and actually offered to pay for the surgery.

He wasn't joking, either. He was dead serious.

I also have a small pet peeve: people telling me that they feel short next to me. Or that my height makes them uncomfortable. What am supposed to do with that? Shall I apologise to you for being tall? Or offer to chop my legs off?

While I was at the post office dropping off mail recently, my back was to an old geezer. He said: 'Wow, what a long ladder you are! I wish I could do what I want with you with every rung I climb.'

I was speechless.

Luckily, one of the women standing in the queue caught him out: 'How dare you! How would you like someone to speak to your daughter that way??'

I was grateful to her and nearly gave her a hug... Still, that was a new low to the list of comments I'd had in my tall life.

#

There were also others who scored points for originality.

In my twenties, when I was toned and fit, someone said: 'Bloody hell, it's Xena!' I had no idea what that meant, until years later when I heard of the Warrior Princess series. I found it hilarious.

Or another one: someone told me with a cheeky grin on their face that they knew why I wore those sunglasses. Well, if you must know, bright light gives me headaches, but I was guessing this was not what that clever boy had in mind. 'So the birds won't fly into your eyes', was his answer. I laughed so hard I nearly peed myself. Good job I have a strong bladder!

Back in Bulgaria, there was one of those guys at the gym who always liked to ask what it was like being tall. I'd make a joke of it and laugh it off, but once decided to tease him back: 'What is it like to be so small, then?'

'It's the breast height to be around you', he didn't miss a beat, and there was a spark of adoration in his eyes. I cracked up laughing.

Another funny one came from one of my English uni mates, a lovely Mexican guy, smiley and cute. I got on with him; he was a kind person. Once, when I came back to England from my Christmas trip to Bulgaria, there was no food left on my shelf in the fridge. Using the same shared kitchen meant that he saw that and looked out for me. He made me an enormous wrap filled with Mexican goodness.

I don't remember being so grateful to many people in my life. He was one of them.

So, he came to me once with this curious smile, and I knew he wasn't going to offend me. He simply wanted to know what I did to grow so tall. What was my secret, was there some sort of giraffe milk?

Not because he wanted to hurt me or to be clever. What he actually wanted was... to be tall!

He, too, had that familiar spark of admiration. Interesting how I'd never seen it with my tall boyfriend, who eventually became my husband!

Realising that I was being admired caught me out. I didn't know how to deal with that.

Which is when I twigged that, perhaps, some short men may actually like tall women. That being as ginormous as me may not necessarily be a flaw. And that, perhaps, if I could somehow learn to accept my height as a fact of life and turn it into an advantage, my world could be a slightly better place.

Short men... The type I never really considered. Why would I? I was only interested in tall men, who, funny enough, never took interest in me. Not that there were many of them, but still. I honestly believed that I was some sort of strong weird magnet for short, big and married men. In all sorts of combinations of these types. What it was that attracted them to me, I had no faintest idea.

Now I, sort of, do. It is, somehow, fashionable nowadays to be with a taller woman. There are all those admirers, fetishists and God knows what else on the World Wide Web. The internet opened a can of worms:

as long as you have any social media account, they are like cockroaches – everywhere. My Instagram and Messenger automatically filter all this crap, so I have no trouble with them, but my new husband freaked out when he found out. Me, I just amuse myself scrolling through them every so often.

I am debating whether to let Alison see this or not. She would probably have a proper field day with these wackos.

This is in a weird way fascinating, really.

I played this little game recently, organised the messages I had in my Messenger and put them in categories. Amusing read. It may seem a bit masochistic keeping all this crap instead of deleting it, but you never know, maybe one day I can compile it all and write some kind of a manual that both ladies and men can read so they can communicate to each other better.

So, just a summary of the most recent ones.

The 'Hello' chat up lines

- *HELLO* (Someone is trying to get my attention – capital letters, eek)
- *Sup*

- *Hi. Hiws u. Hows u*

- *Hi. There?*

- *Hi … can I ask you question ?*

- *Hey Victoria can I talk to you*

- *Hola linda*

- *Hi tall lady*

- *Hii beautiful*

- *Hii beautiful lady how r u*

- *Hello Add me Please Okey*

- *hello. disturb?*

The height related chat up lines

- *Hi. excuse me. how tall are you?*

- *are you a tall girl? omg*

- *Hi R u tall girl*

- *Size 11? Really? Oops:)*

- *Hey what shoe size r u?*

- *How tall are you miss ?*

- *Hello 6'5 ½ woman* (This one actually bothered doing his homework!)

- *Hello Victoria. And Thank you. You ré taller Than me lol*

- *Hi it me if u like short man iam here I want ti talk with u !*

- *How tall are u*

- *You're tall as me :-D :-D :-D*

- *hieee. dear. h r u. u look very tall*

- *Hello i'm chris , would you like to use one of my stereo decks some weeks to relax your bare feet on it and rub and massage your bare feet over it a lot and even stand on it barefoot please ,i would love to have lot of bare feetmarks on it and your feetsmell please you not have to care if it get dammaged by your strong feet even if you dammage it slowly with your bare feet for your own fun and use it to pose on it barefoot for pics would be great too i love big female feet on my stereo , they can easy handle it*

- *hi victoria how tall are you lol*

The admiration chat up lines

- *wow nice*

- *Cok guzelsin Victoria* (Hm, I guess one more nationality I could pass for could possibly be Turkish, so – granted, good try)

- *U r cute*

- *princess good name*

- *Hi , I saw ur pic , u r beautiful , if u like u can send Mssge , my wechat , tango , whatsapp , viber and skype are...*
- *Hi Victoria , love your height your such a hottie*
- *Very sexy lady*
- *I don't usually do this but this time I just had to*
- *Your'resume a nice looking 6'5 ½ lady Victoria*
- *wow gorgeous. how tall are you?*

If she doesn't respond, she is not interested – but let's try again... and again... and again!

- *U thr.* A month later: *'Hi'.* Another week later: *'Hi'.* 10 months later: *'Hi. How tall r u'.* Two more months later: *'Hi'.* At what point will he get the idea I am not really interested?
- *Hello you is well.* A month later – same question, no improvement in grammar: *'Hello you is well Victoria'*
- *Hello can I ask you a question??* (and two hours later: '??')
- *please add me.* 3 months later: *'Hello, please reply me'*
- *Hi miss Victoria. How are you?* (sent in July). *Hi miss tall gilr how are you? How tall are you?* (February the following year) *hi miss im niko nice to meet you.* (November)

- *Hi how r u. How tall u r ?* (June). *Hi how r u* (11 days later). *Hi* (the following day). *Hi. Hello* (July). *Hi. How r u* (August). *Hi. U thrre* (November). *Can we chat* (in another couple of days). *Hi how r u. U there. U there.* (fucking October the following year). No word since then. I wonder if he may have got the message... or died??

- *hi i am from india & iam 5.8 tall men & i like tall girls. how tall you, pls add me* (January) *good morning how are you. i am sports teacher from India. i am big fan of tall girls pls add me* (December)

- *Hey gorgeous. There?* Five days later: *'!?'*

- *Love your profile picture you look great love the height difference I'm 5ft6 you are 6ft?* (May) *Hi Victoria whats it like being a tall women in a mans world i'm 5ft5 tall and a man* (June) *Hi Victoria love your height of 6ft5 ½ awesome* (July) *Hi Victoria your legs look enormouly long in the dress from phase eight you look great* (a few days later)

- *Hi* (December) *Hi Victoria* (December again) *Hallo* (June the following year) *Hallo* (July)

- *Helloooo* (July) *Hello* (three weeks later) *Helloo* (July)

I even got a poem (which, no doubt, would have also been sent to a number of other tall women around the globe):

pritty is beauty no beauty is pretty no pritty is no beauty love is beauty loving is beautful living is good understandi ng is the best your eyes are like ice when it melts it is cool water it makes every one feel cool so you make every one cool and make everybody happy your smile is ur look your looks is ur smile your eyes are like moon in the sky your lookway down is like lighting in sky and your way of approch is like me in the heaven and the way you talk it like sweet hope is poem is good when i look at you i have to look up to you.

Next time I go to Alison, I bring along a printed copy of all this crap. Reading her facial expressions: highly entertaining!

She doesn't need to say anything. I can see it – *now* she gets it: what it really is to be a tall woman. I may not quite be the tallest woman in the world, but it certainly feels like it, reading all this.

Life's Dilemma: Shorter Men

When I was younger, I always thought I'd die single. Yes, I wasn't social – granted. I wasn't the prettiest, either – granted. And I was more intelligent than most boys I met, which didn't help. But it was my freaking height that stopped me from looking at anyone shorter than me in *that* way. Plus, in the nineties, there weren't many tall men around in Bulgaria, anyway. All we could do to meet people was bump into them in real life. Facebook wasn't invented yet. Or dating websites – just because there was no such thing as the Internet.

Naturally, I always felt that my choice was made for me already. Pre-determined, sort of. Or, to say it in other words, I was doomed. Fucked.

It is not like I had many tall girlfriends either to exchange notes with, so I had to trust my own judgement – which was always strongly against embarrassing myself of even thinking of dating anyone shorter than me.

Even for a therapist, understanding my tall issues takes some work, as they are not on the radar of someone who is on the short side. We talk about it in detail and Alison shows some real interest in what I have to say. Feels as if she has found a gold mine. Yes, she got to the bottom of it. At last.

Which reminds me just why I have always felt that being tall has messed up my whole life. I felt that my life choices were made for me already. I wasn't an ordinary teenage girl flirting with boys – because I was far too tall for them. I wasn't interested in sex – because there was no one around to spark that interest off in me, they were all far too short to interest me.

On the other hand, I used to get regularly hit on by older (shorter, obviously) boys and men. They assumed I was older than I was, even when I was a pre-teen, and made advances to me. I found that gross.

I feel sometimes as if I have been robbed of something. Having no actual choice of boys of my size, and later on – men, deprived me from what most girls had: frivolous, happy youth, flirting, feeling wanted. Which doesn't mean I would have liked to be a whore, but being chased by boys makes you a different kind of person. One that loves herself... instead of hating her body.

Yes, I hated being tall. For far too many reasons, and a major one of them was lack of choice in boys. And men. Which is most likely why I ended up making the wrong choice of man to marry. Just because someone was tall, clever and took interest in me, I felt that was the opportunity of a lifetime for me. After all, there are not many men who ticked all those boxes, so I went all in.

And one day I discovered Facebook and all those groups of tall people. The curtain was lifted: there were other people on this planet who felt like me!

Feeling validated was such a relief. I joined as many groups as I could find, and hungrily drunk in any posts they'd put up, just to realise that so many more people struggled with the same issues I always had.

I wasn't the only tall woman who didn't like her height!

But what a shock it was to find out that there was another side of the story that I never suspected: tall women did actually dare go out with shorter men. And were... happy!

In a moment of self-doubt, I decided to ask those virtual tall fellows the big question: would they date shorter guys? The answers came flooding in. Not the kind of responses I was expecting, though.

There was more to life than being with a man of your height. I painfully scrolled through all answers and my eyes, reluctantly, started welling up.

Fuck that! Have I missed out on finding real love just because I let my height define me?

I took some sad pleasure in dissecting people's opinions... while also contemplating my own tall life. The one I chose to live in misery and prejudice because of my height... which didn't stop other people from being happy.

I felt I had to document all this. The academic in me raised her head and, meticulously, got analysing – in the vague hope that she may have got it wrong.

Nope. The comments kept coming in.

All these women said they were happy to be with a shorter partner...

- *I felt comfortable. I liked it.*

- *I'm 6'3". My husband is 6'. He is my protector. It's all in a man's attitude or how he carries himself. He is definitely an Alpha male. That's why we work together! It takes a man that's very secure in his masculinity to be with a taller woman.*

- *I am 6'1". Shortest man I've ever had a date with – 5'1". You have to maintain your sense of humour and the man definitely has to be a secure person. It definitely draws attention – not like I need any help.*

And not shallow. The struggle is real to not feel like you are huge when it is a small man you are on a date with.

- *I dated a couple of short guys. One 5' 4", one 5' 6". They loved that I was 6'. One wanted me to wear heels. If I had really cared for them, their height wouldn't have mattered.*
- *Dated plenty of shorter blokes. Only a problem if he has a problem. Never an issue for me. Sometimes other people laugh. Who cares!?*

I stop in shock. She did not care! Why did I have to always care what people thought? Why did I have to please everyone? And why was I afraid of not fitting in?

- *Yes, if you are happy to constantly be analysed by others and asked the same tedious questions day in, day out.*
- *There is a 5" difference between me and my husband. We've been married 17 years. If I want a tall hug, he just stands up the stairs a step.*
- *I personally don't care about height in a relationship. If we have good chemistry, that's all that matters.*

Chemistry... Now, that's a thought. Not something I have thought about... ever.

- *Been with my amazing 5'9" husband for 25 years. I'm 6'. Don't make height an issue. Love is the best protector.*

- *I'm 6'3", dated a few guys who were an inch shorter, but generally it has always been 6'5 ½ guys. If the guy is shorter, he's gotta have a great charisma and massive confidence.*

- *It feels weird. I feel like the men and lots of people stare but I don't want to potentially miss out on an amazing person because of shallow reasons. The shortest was 12 cm shorter than me.*

- *I'm 6' and my partner is 5'8". He is very comfortable with my height and our height difference – to the point that he is happy for me to wear heels if we go out.*

- *I had a partner for nearly 8 years who was 5'8" and I'm 6'3". Didn't bother us. But is REALLY nice to have a partner the same height. We fit together better. In more ways than one!*

- *I am 6'1" and dating guys who are 5'6"-5'7" many times. It is actually very sexy for me to take on the not usual role... be in the more dominant side and just feel like a goddess.*

- *I always liked being with shorter guys.*

Why, just why, did I not ever think of a shorter man being a possibility?

Strictly speaking, I did, but simply through lack of choice. So it happened that my first man *was* a bit shorter than me. Only a couple of centimetres, though, so it didn't bother me. After him, I never looked down. Which, now, turns out to have been one of the biggest mistakes in my life. That could have prevented my major failure in love.

Anyway, what did men have to say? Maybe that would validate my feelings and show me that they are repulsed by the very idea of being with a woman taller than them?

The vast majority of men, actually, shared their love and admiration for women like me.

- *I'd love to find a woman taller than myself.*
- *Sure, I'm 5'10" and the taller women I've dated all felt protected in my presence. I carry total confidence and power in my personality, I've been told. In the end they never had a problem with my height, even if* they *might have in the beginning.*
- *I dig tall women, but I rarely see them out. But I'd definitely date a tall woman!*
- *I am 5'10", and I usually date women taller than me. I love the attention we get. Very comfortable and used to it.*

• *These women one day will understand that their focus on height only hurts their love life. Love, the right love is what matters. Not how you feel or perceive his ability to protect based on height. A taller man gives no more security because he is tall. Common sense should overrule that inaccurate feeling. Good luck out there, tall ladies!*

This last one has me in tears.

Fuck. Me. I am such a loser.

<u>Failure Six. Love</u>

My mother always told me off for the way I held a broom. Our family functioned in the dark ages as far as technology was concerned: any equipment had to be as old and simple as possible, and God forbid that anyone might have wanted to buy anything new to replace it!

I didn't use a vacuum cleaner, but that old fashion witches' mode of transportation, and was happy enough with that. Looking at various memes on Facebook subtly suggesting that all women should ride brooms, I'd quite fancy using one of these, actually! After all, my kids refer to me sometimes as a witch – and they don't mean it in a nasty way! I can see how healing with my hands and doing distant Reiki sessions to people may be seen as a witch's ability.

I recently mentioned to my son that, strangely, my right knee had started hurting, and it happened the day after I'd given Reiki to his stepdad's right knee. This is what I have witnessed happening with mediums, but is also not uncommon amongst energy healers. Nick's interest peaked and he decided to try me and check if I'd be able to guess his thoughts. Funny enough, I did. I even managed to guess what number he was thinking of, which properly freaked him out. My husband, too, says sometimes that yup, I am, actually, a witch. Who am I to argue with that: his mum had certain paranormal abilities, so maybe he knows better than me?

Wishful thinking. If only I were a proper witch, I'd have, by now, wiped off my entire credit card balance and got everyone in my life, hubby included, to play ball, rather than irritate me and stress me out.

Yes, I think it may be time to call things what they are and admit that, well, yes, perhaps I am pretty stressed at times. Or... more often than not.

So, all things considered, I could really use a broom and just sod off, leaving everyone else to sort themselves out without me having to try and clone myself, to do everything they expect from me and be everywhere when I am needed at the same time. Like that book I devoured a few years ago, where I may well have been the main character: 'I Don't Know How She Does It'. Neither do I, I just do it.

My husband says this comes with the territory of being a mum. I'd say it comes with a different territory: being a people pleaser, to the point when you are not doing yourself any favours. For which, I guess, I should be blaming my mum. If she hadn't had such high expectations of me, perhaps I could have turned up a bit more laid back.

Anyway, she wouldn't get tired of reminding me just how to use this important household tool – while in my eyes, a broom was a broom, and that was all there was to it: it just swept up the rubbish. No rocket science, really. I hated hoovering, so whenever I could get away with it, I'd sweep the floor instead of faffing around with the vacuum cleaner that was easily my parents' age and just as noisy as the whole traffic on the busy boulevard we lived above. Trying to manoeuvre the damn prehistoric thing and listen to its efforts to overpower the buses outside: kill – me – now!

'Remember! You *must* sweep *away* from you, not *towards* you! Otherwise you will never get married!' God forbid.

Sweep away from you and you will live happily ever after!

I'd roll my eyes and carry on sweeping in whichever way felt comfortable at the time. Whether or not I used the broom in the correct direction, I was doomed, anyway, so may as well not bother!

Yes, I always thought I'd die single. Or, what could be even worse – a virgin. Not only because I knew I wasn't exactly beautiful – although there was that, too.

Why I was convinced I'd end up as an old spinster was the same reason for pretty much everything else that had gone wrong in my life:

my excessive height. We already know that I never looked at a man in *that* way unless he was my size... which, in those days when I had to be out and about living my life and dating hot guys, wasn't so easy. Even nowadays, with the surge of tall youngsters in the new generations, it would have been quite a job to find a decent boy of my height – while here, we are talking late eighties. Zero chance!

Not that there weren't any tall boys around: you could meet the random one every so often. My choice was limited by one more factor, though: their brains. Now, the combination of these two requirements was pretty rare to find. To also expect for someone who ticked those two boxes to show any vaguest interest in me meant one thing: winning the lottery would have probably been a bit more realistic, at least in those days. In this modern day and age, possibly slightly less so. Although one could argue.

Perhaps I was born in the wrong decade. Or century, even.

Otherwise, over the course of my younger life, I did have some encounters with tall men. Just because there weren't too many of them, I can still remember each one. Mind you, I lived in a half-a-million city!

There was this guitar player in a band I hung around with. Man, was he hot! He had this body that would drive every girl bonkers, sexy thin fingers and amazing hair: longer and, probably, shinier and better conditioned than mine. His intelligence? The size of an aspirin.

There was also that economist guy who used to pay me random visits in the office: he was, nearly, the required height. Although not quite, but perhaps close enough for me to consider going out with him. Well, he was as shy as a whatsit, and never dared make eye contact with me. I couldn't say I fancied him or anything, but he was vaguely tall and convincingly intelligent, so I felt compelled to show interest in him. I thought he liked me, but being the geek that he was, never managed to do anything about it. I saw him walking with his parents once, and that finally killed it for me. He must have felt the vibes, as I never saw him in my office ever again.

Or... that guitar player. I met him at uni, through the jazz band playing in their soundproof underground premises, hazy with the smoke of fags and probably something else which, then, was a smell I wasn't familiar with. As usual, I'd meet a band to interview them for the local papers, and then become friends with them.

These were the times when I started coming out of my shell and meeting boys. Simply because we had a shared interest in music – not because I was 'interested' in them, or they in me. I was too tall to even think about any of that. Perhaps this is exactly why we spent so much time together: they knew I wasn't with them with the secret hope to bed them; I was actually interested in their music, and they appreciated that. I helped them by being their informal publicist in the big city, and this made me somehow equal, as opposed to meat for sex. I had their respect, and it had nothing to do with my height. I was liked for who I was.

So, this guy... He was my first real crush. Oh, his forearms! I still swallow hard thinking about them. He used to roll his sleeves up, light up a cigarette and talk to me through the smoke about William Faulkner. Or was it Charles Bukowski? It was me who was fonder of Faulkner, while he was all about being a roamer. A bohemian – which I would never dare consider, not with my upbringing. I never got Bukowski. Living on the road didn't do it for me – but sounded so sexy coming from the mouth of this young and tall sex on legs. As a figure of speech, of course, as I knew nothing of sex.

A couple of years ago I found out he'd been living in London for the past few months. I thought it was now safe enough to have a chat with him without entering any dangerous territories: my passion for him had died and, in the process, I'd proven to be a good friend and a capable rock journalist for the local Bulgarian scene. So, I didn't think much of it when

I decided to mock myself by mentioning that I once had a secret crush on him... twenty odd years ago.

'Yes, I know... I knew all along'. His voice sounded deeper than usual. Me, I was breathless.

Shit. Just how embarrassing could it get? I was sure I never showed I fancied him. I even got close with the girl who soon became his girlfriend. I remembered blushing hard while listening to her stories of how she visited him in the army (there was compulsory military service for all young men in the post-communist bloc), how they explored each other's sexuality, not knowing what to do and how to relieve their virgin's frustrations... Those were probably the most embarrassing conversations I'd ever had with a girlfriend, simply because I had a crush on the very boy she was going out with.

I still feel a tad proud for befriending her. As painful as it was to start with, she was one of the best friends I ever had. And, somehow, she never found out about my crush on her boyfriend!

Apparently, he actually did. How pathetic.

I still have a weak spot for masculine forearms. With a bit of hair: just about enough to cover them, not too thick or dark. Gives me goose bumps.

So, men in my life: sad story.

On the other hand, though, there was a silver lining – as always. Remember, it is not about what happens to you, but how you respond to it!

Om.

Yes, silver lining: I had such amazing male friends!

#

When I read all those Facebook comments from short guys, I started to wonder if some of these fantastic friends I had may have actually had a crush on me – but never considered asking me out, for the same reason it didn't cross my mind, either. After all, we lived in the same old fashioned society.

Catch 22.

Maybe that's why I got so uncomfortable during the rehearsal of one of the local heavy metal bands I was friends with. Their long and messy haired singer was having a chat with me, leaning onto some dodgy balustrade with some kind of aplomb that I vaguely registered but didn't think twice about. No idea what we talked about, no doubt about some renegade lyrics, or about the shit of post-communist hypocrisy we lived in, or who knows what else. His voice sounded huskier than usual. I still remember his inquisitive look, the intense blue colour of his eyes, and feeling lost in them. I didn't understand just why I felt so hot and bothered. He couldn't have fancied me, after all: with his lovely wife waiting for him, but mostly, with these centimetres in his height seriously missing.

Now I know: yes, he did desperately fancy me, just never told me. He loved his wife – granted. But men are like that. They can be pigs and take what they can, if they can. He would have gladly dragged me to bed that night after rehearsal. And he didn't care that I was taller than him. Height does not matter in bed.

Good job I had no idea. Now, that would have been another serious mistake to make! Once in my life is quite enough.

So, here is one thing that my parents did manage to achieve: to make sex look out of reach for me for far longer than it should have been. It was never on their radar and, somehow, this is how it was for me.

'You don't have sex for pleasure', lectured my mum, again. This time in anger, when she first found out I'd slept with a man. I was in my mid-twenties. 'You only have sex to have children!'

Again, I knew better than trying to argue with this.

I was twenty five when I was with a man for the first time. The longer I was being a virgin, the more it seemed like something I just could not do.

Where did all this come from? From my parents? Partly, maybe. Largely, for another reason: my height complex.

I could have probably had any man I wanted. If only I wanted it. If only I could come out of my books and look at real life around me.

I did have a smashing body, just didn't know it. I had a great personality for my age, but didn't know that, either. I thought of myself as a geek. I was too shy and too busy being tall.

This is why I must bring my daughter up differently. She should know that she is amazing as she is. If she wants to be with someone, they don't have to be as tall as her. I have to help her be different from me. I need to fix what my mum did not for me.

As far as my life was concerned, an old Bulgarian proverb sums it up: best apples are eaten by the pigs. What I'd add to that is: because they are so tall that they don't know they are the best.

So, as already established, I lived in a society that followed traditional norms. Girls were the shorter ones in a couple, and that was that.

Sometimes, complete strangers would comment on how hard it must be for me to find dates. They would say that with a pitiful, almost worried, expression... Others – in a purely sarcastic manner. Like any other comments about my height, I'd just ignore them. Until, finally, it got to me. First of all, what is it to you, and how dare you bluntly poke your nose into my personal life? And, secondly, being tall is not a disfigurement! I am a woman in my own rights: same as everyone else, just a bit taller. Or yes, a lot taller than the rest. But I am a fully functioning, thinking and feeling, human being.

Those stupid pity comments made me want to bury my head in the sand. Or, rather, bang theirs against the wall!

Anyway, yes, it has been hard for me to date, but that, it turned out, was through my own choice...

And what a wrong choice that may have been.

But, again, there is a silver lining. Choosing to only take interest in tall guys made me different – again. I chose to do other things with my life.

Being tall made me who I am. This is why I excelled in my studies. This is why I had such a high flying career (back in Bulgaria, that is). This is why I buried myself in books and writing. Because I was trying to compensate for the lack of something I desperately wanted but would not admit to myself: love.

Which everyone deserves. Regardless of their height.

Finding comfort in reading and writing resulted in one of my major failures: a dream and potential that never happened. I never made it as a journalist, or a writer. But it helped me overcompensate for my lack of a boyfriend. For that alone, it should have been a good thing.

When I worked long hours, I kept saying to myself: I wasn't a career freak, I was simply single. That evening when we were budgeting for a new project at 11 p.m., I reckoned with myself: one day when I have a boyfriend or family, I would prioritise them before my career. Which is exactly what happened. Ironically, not through my own choice – but because my husband did not want me to have a career. Career was just satisfaction to a woman's ego. Her place was at home: in the kitchen and looking after children. Work was just to pay the bills.

This had nothing to do with my height.... But I ended up in that relationship because of one simple factor: my husband was taller than me.

I know now: you don't marry someone for their height. I didn't know it then. I considered myself very lucky because someone tall and intelligent enough showed interest in me. This ticked all my three boxes that I didn't think would ever happen. This was as good as it'd ever get, and I had to grab this opportunity.

Today, I am married for a second time. To a tall man. Again.

Am I repeating the same mistake? Quite possibly, judging by our not too perfect relationship. Is it possible to find everything in a man who just happens to be tall?

Or maybe I just shot myself in the foot – again. Fuck knows. Love is just not one of my successes.

Why My Best Friends Are Short

After having to deal with the grim memories of my love life, today Alison has decided to take a different direction. Do I want to contemplate my other relationships, like my friends? For a change, I do! I love my friends, I miss them, and I don't often get the chance to talk about them. I nearly feel like grabbing a coffee with her this morning, but hold this suggestion back... It feels childish, and very inappropriate.

For a second, an uncomfortable thought visits my head: have I become a bit too close with my therapist? She knows so many of my secrets and intimate thoughts... I wonder if she has worked me out by now. Does she have an agenda of some sort that I am not aware of?

I brush those thoughts off. This must be my history talking: always being defensive and expecting that people will criticise me or bully me. Like a hedgehog, having my spikes out for protection.

No, she has no agenda other than to help me feel happier in myself. Don't be paranoid, Vick.

I am guessing the picture I have portrayed of myself must be of a loner... Yes, I like my own company, but this is because I am hardly ever alone! Plus, the things I like doing cannot really be done together with another person, like sleeping for ten hours, or reading, or listening to new music and then writing my reviews, or meditating with Reiki, or a yoga session where I choose my flow depending on what my body needs on that particular day. Although with yoga, and with aerobics for that matter, I do enjoy being part of a group: it has a special vibe to it, endorphins keep flying off the charts, but as far as yoga is concerned, I get the kick from it, mentally and emotionally, when I practise alone. Cooking is also best done alone, as too many nannies can spoil the broth, or however the saying went.

Other than that, once my 'me time' needs have been satisfied, I am actually quite a social bunny. Not as in going clubbing and shopping, or any of that. I am more of a 'meet over coffee or lunch' kind of girl, as this is when you get those meaningful conversations going.

For us, friendship is more than going to the cinema together. As a matter of fact, that is in an activity I prefer if I don't want to converse with someone: you just stare at a screen together; any comments, and people shush at you! Being friends is about knowing and helping each other through life, which is why going for a walk or having coffee is a much better choice. Now, with my height, the first option is not too clever, as it gives me neck pain looking down, and same for my friends –

looking up to me. Sat down is what we prefer, for that sole reason. And for our shared love of coffee and cake!

As our clothes and shoe sizes are different, the likelihood of chit chatting about shopping (what we got and where from) is pretty much non-existent. We acknowledge each other's new buys ('Hey, I love your new coat, hun!' sort of thing), but we won't make this the main topic of a conversation. Not that there's anything wrong with having a fashion conversation, or a rant about the lack of fashion resources for us, tall girls, but, after all, there are far more important things that connect us. We can talk about many other things – and so we do.

I forget that I am tall for a moment and chat about stuff that interests 'normal' people.

I like talking! And, boy, do I talk!

But only when the other person is interested in what I have to say. Genuinely interested, that is! Otherwise, I just clam up and mind my own business. This is my life lesson from Valentina's times, when our conversations were a one way street and anything I had to say was dismissed as uninteresting. At least I learnt from that: I know now to look for signs of whether I should talk or not, so mostly try to keep my mouth shut and stay out of trouble. Which is not good for my mental health, I am guessing, as bottling things up may cause more harm than not.

After those fifteen years of marriage, I felt rather uninteresting: my ex-husband didn't like chit chatting. No such thing as talking about what I wanted to get off my chest. All he was interested in was stuff that directly concerned us as a family.

I am a different person now, closer to my real self. And free to use my mouth much more!

So, I do have friends. Quite a few, as a matter of fact. I don't get to see them a lot, particularly the ones from my Bulgarian years – because of the simple geographical side of things. We are scattered all over the globe. There was that one Christmas break, though, when we all, magically, went back to Bulgaria to see our families, and, somehow, I set my own all-time record of how many friends I could meet in two weeks. Not because I had the intention to go for 'quantity'; it's just how things turned out. Nick was at an age when his grandparents quite enjoyed spending time with him, so they took over completely and left me at my own devices.

I met fifteen of my friends during that break. Fifteen! I didn't even know I had that many! And this wasn't all of them... They were all good friends of mine, busy with their own lives across thousands of miles around the globe.

'Are any of them tall?' Alison asks with a slight spike of curiosity.

Interesting enough, none of them are, as a matter of fact! The corners of my therapist's eye smile. Her face stays straight but it does soften up. She feels the love I am radiating and I can see she likes it.

Alison seems quite interested to hear about my friends, which in turn takes me by surprise. Have I projected myself as that much of an introvert?

#

There is no particular reason why all my best friends are short. It simply happens: mainly because there are not many tall girls that I know, and somehow with the ones I do, we just don't click. After all, we pick our friends for reasons other than their size, so just because they are closer to my height, that doesn't mean I should be BFFs with them.

A bit like being friends with Bulgarians in the UK: just because we share the same nationality, that doesn't mean we will necessarily get along. Right?

My best friends don't care about my height. Or my weight, for that matter. They won't ask me all those questions that drive me nuts. The one of the sort of 'Just how tall are you exactly?'; 'Do you think I am tall?' and stuff. It makes no difference to them whatsoever, as all they care about is my friendship and whether our characters click. Same goes for me. Interestingly, my best friends are usually (a tad) overweight. Iva, the girl who ended up being a lawyer, has always had her own struggles: being like a yo-yo, on and off diets, and never finding anyone in life – not just because she is always late (which surely doesn't help!), but also because she is quite a large girl, and that gives her plenty of insecurities similar to mine.

Which is perhaps why we feel similar: having our own body struggles and hang ups. We help each other's self-esteem and pick each other up. This is why we are best friends. We are always there for each other – even when we are 2,000 odd miles apart.

Same with my other best and good friends. It may have something to do with the fact that we met in our very young years when we were all growing. I was, once, their size, but over time they saw me change into this giantess that I am now. They grew at the same time as me, just at a different rate, which probably helped them see me as one of them, rather than someone different.

They never discuss my height; not even when we meet after many years of being away from each other – with the odd exception of humorous comments like 'Oh, I'd forgotten how tall you were!' Which is fair enough; they had to adjust their head and neck position to meet my eyes, but that was about it.

Our relationships never changed over the years: height is not relevant in our friendship's world.

Alison regards me with a more obvious smile: 'I am guessing, there was not much competition over men in that case, given your height differences?'

Which is another good point; this is the ultimate advantage of having a friend totally opposite your size. It is very common for tall men to date short girls, but not in the circle of my friends. Knowing just how limited my choice is by my height, my besties wouldn't even think of getting in the way. They had plenty of options of their own.

#

There are a few tall women in my wider friend's circle, but somehow they never made it into the 'Best Friends' category.

Cynically speaking, competition over men could well be a reason why we don't get along. That friend of mine with the pregnancy scare dream, she was nearly 190 cm tall, and we know already what happened. While trying to fix me up with that ever so tall basketball player (who became my first official boyfriend), she hooked up with his brother... who was so hot that it was him I actually fancied in the first place, but she very quickly snapped him.

Which comes to show that I couldn't be trusted, either! Where is that sisterhood that the Cosmopolitan bangs on about?? It is much safer to be best friends with someone you would not be in competition with! Plus, that friend had a much better body than me. For a start, her hips were not as ginormous, and, more importantly, she was happy to have sex with him pretty much from date number one. While me, this was not something I felt ready for... and very soon Ivan lost interest in me for that reason.

Years down the line, that same friend admitted that the guy she actually fancied in the first place was the brother I ended up with. Perhaps that's why I never trusted her: I took a fancy of her boyfriend, and she – of mine? Talking about girls' solidarity! Nah, not when you are both tall with a limited choice of men. Our height was the actual cause of this entire drama, getting us to compete over the few available tall guys. Pathetic or what.

What an irony: we both ended up with the wrong brother and, logically, both split up with them. Isn't life strange.

How do normal women live in this world full of men and choice?? That, actually, sounds pretty scary! Perhaps being limited in my options wasn't such a bad thing after all... Less choice – fewer disappointments!

There was also this girl who started up a modelling agency back in Bulgaria. She asked me once for my measurements. They appeared to be perfect – to my own surprise, and hers. She quickly concluded, though: 'No, you are too tall to be a model. I won't be able to find you a partner on stage. Sorry, chick!'

Funny enough, she was very tall herself. Other than that, though, as much as she was a lovely girl, we hardly had anything else in common.

I also have a clever tall friend in London. She is a high flying career woman that I admire a lot. Which means I hardly have anything in common with her, either: I always compare myself to her and see what I don't have. Cannot have. Like courage and money. Perfect body, boob job and an attractive tall hunk for a husband. Some do have it all!

I also had a few tall male friends, which was tricky. Somehow, to me someone being tall automatically meant my interest peaks by default. I am surprised I didn't end up having a crush on them. How *do* other women choose in this sea of men??

For a brief second, I imagine that I was shorter, so could potentially have any man I met, not just those taller than me. Hm.... I think it may be better off counting my blessings, thanks.

There is one thing, though, that I am missing out on by not hanging out with other tall girls: shopping. Wouldn't it be nice to mooch around the shops like normal girls do, and *then* grab that coffee? Well, no, for two reasons. One: all my tall friends live too far away, and two: there are no shops we can go to for clothes to fit us. Otherwise, it would be nice to have someone who can give you shopping advice, if you need one – but this is what Facebook groups are for! It would also be nice to have someone to swap shoes and clothes with, like in the movies.

Never gonna happen!

Instead, what I get is conversations like this.

Me: 'Oh, I desperately need a new pair of jeans. Long Tall Sally have closed down, so I have no idea where to go now. I am so fed up with ordering from various websites, then waiting, hoping they'll fit, only to send them back because they are too short!'

My shorter friend: 'Ah, I know where! I bought some from Zara/Marks and Spencer's/Next/you name it, and they were really long! Have you tried there??'

Me (sighing, deeply, while trying to suppress my frustration and, actually, irritation): 'Yeah, I have. They are too short.'

My friend: 'But they were *really* long on me! And I am 5'8"!'

I wonder whether I should laugh or cry. How is 5'8" anything remotely tall?? I still try to smile and brush her ideas off politely. After all, she is a good friend and is only trying to help, so doesn't deserve attitude and stuff.

Me, again: 'I know. They won't fit, trust me. Too short.'

She: 'Honestly, they were huge! You really should try! We can go shopping together, how about that? Wouldn't it be nice to have a break from online shopping?'

I seriously try not to roll my eyes at her. I don't want to be rude... But she just doesn't get the message: no fucking shops sell jeans that have a 1 percent chance of fitting me. None. Zero. Nil.

Me (finding the last ounces left of my sense of humour): 'Yes, that would be lovely! But I've had these legs for a long time, you know, so I have tried it all. Literally, all! Honest!'

My friend just fucking doesn't want to give up: 'Well, let's go to the shops and see?'

I know she is trying to help, I know! But she has just no concept of what it is like to be a giantess like me with freakishly long legs. Yeah, I know that Tesco's jeans are 34 inch inner leg. Cool, innit. Just I need a 38, not 34, so please, just drop it. Let's not ruin our friendships over things we can do nothing about.

So, here... the joy of being best friends with girls who are a foot shorter than me. Ish.

The Colour of My Hair

It was a regular evening after work. The only deviation from the norm was stopping at Aldi for some groceries. Only just briefly, of course; there is never time for shopping therapy on a weekday evening.

I always make a point of going in and out as quick as I can. Those buggers waiting for me at home don't just need me to have their dinner cooked, but, mainly, as a referee. The sooner I get back home, the less are the chances I'd find that a nuclear explosion has blasted my family apart, and the less likelihood there is I'd catch my hubby packing his bags after snapping my son's head off.

Sigh. Concentrate on the bloody shopping, and nothing bad will happen. They will survive another twenty minutes without me.

The lady at the checkout looked at me with some interest. I felt uneasy – what was wrong with me?? Apart from being (permanently) tall – obviously, but I somehow knew there was another reason for her curiosity.

'Are you OK for bags?' she asked, while I was rummaging through my handbag.

Yes, I was. I detest paying pennies for reusable bags, but also I do try to make some contributions to saving the planet by using my own. Recycling maniac and all...

'I like the colour of your hair!' she blurted out, just like that. Now, that wasn't your typical British female!

She was a lady in her late fifties – sixties, perhaps; looking at me kindly, with the sort of warmth that you would only expect from a close friend. This woman didn't *have* to be nice to me. All she had to do was scan my groceries and take my money. I had no choice but to smile at her. It felt disarming.

It was one of those lousy days where the last thing I felt like was talking to strangers. I'd been worn out by the heavy combination of office politics, workload and commute.

I am all for women's solidarity, OK. For Christ sakes, I subscribe to the Cosmopolitan! Have been for fifteen years or so. We need to help each other out; sisterhood and all. Not that I've had other women do it to me much, but I will regularly pay compliments on someone's clothes, accessories, whatever. Not necessarily because I genuinely like them! I'd just pick up when someone needs that extra bit of attention. Every so often, my intuition would poke me: 'Here, this girl could do with a smile, or a nice word. Go on, do it!' I guess you could say that was the empath in me raising her head.

Which is exactly what this woman did: she lifted me up.

'I really like it!' she demanded, 'What make is it?'

This is when she got all my attention. I gleamed and engaged in the conversation fully. I hardly recognised myself. I never do this kind of chit chat!

She was genuinely interested, and this took me aback. I knew exactly what brand the hair dye was, but, just then, couldn't remember the exact details.

'L'Oréal something... Cream colour... Not sure what it's called, actually.'

'It is an unusual shade, too!' she continued. It was clear that she did mean what she said, which pleased me even more. It felt genuine, and I liked the attention. At the same time, I blushed, wondering just how pathetic I could get. Someone made me a compliment, and I was all in. Was I *that* desperate?

The thing is, the colour *was* unusual. I bought it in error... as I do. My absentmindedness has improved a lot, but I still make the odd stupid mistake. I am only human. I thought this was my regular shade, dark brown. It turned out it was 'ruby black'. When I realised I'd got the wrong colour, I couldn't help thinking of all those horrific stories about hair dye experiments gone bad. Back in the day, the girl who did my hair in Bulgaria sent me off to the local supply shop once, instructing me to get myself a particular hair dye... in blonde. I have always been a brunette. So, hairdressers know better; that dye gave my hair a lovely chestnut colour, after all. Still, what the hell *was* ruby black?

It turned out to be a successful experiment after all. Needless to say, no one noticed my new colour. Hubby wouldn't anyway, but even Nick (usually very observant) didn't notice the change of shade either.

And there she was: a complete stranger admiring my hair, being friendly and trying to get as much information about my hair dye as she could. Good job I had quite a few items on the conveyor belt, otherwise I'd have got on the fellow buyers' nerves! She also wanted to know where I got it from, which, in return, made me want to be helpful in appreciation of her friendliness. I magically remembered that I bought it at Boots, as a matter of fact, and even exactly how much it cost on a special offer.

Walking away from the till, I knew this had made my day. The nameless lady made me feel special at a time when I wasn't. She made the world seem right again. I forgot about the shitty commute and my colleague's snappy comments. For a change, I looked forward to going back into the battlefield at home. I felt appreciated, although in a weird and unusual sort of way.

This came at the end of long six months when I'd resolved to not dying my hair at all – for as long as I could. My husband had always been affirming that he didn't find grey hair unsexy. Until then, I kept dying it regularly, and I did it for myself, not for him. Or so I thought.

He hadn't said a word about my awfully grown grey roots – credit given where it's due. If that were my first husband, I'd have been ridiculed as hell, as already happened on the one occasion when I left my hair undyed for six unbelievable months. I was actually starting to get used to it. I did it, funny enough, following his mother's suggestion (bitch!!): 'You know you had highlights in your hair last year? It would be much better if you wait until it all grows back undyed, and then have blonde streaks put in. It will blend it with your natural greys and will look better!'

I still wonder if she did it to set me up. At the time, I thought she meant well, so duly followed her advice... Until her son snapped at me one day: 'What the fuck are you trying to achieve, remind me that you are older than me or what?? When *will* you dye your hair at last??'

I was four years older than him. I never felt the age difference between us. Until that day. After that, I never forgot it.

Since that incident, I'd never let my hair grow for so long without dying it – until now. Don't know why I decided to do it; just thought I'd give my hair a break from chemicals or something. Funny enough, an ad popped up in my Facebook feed just then (as it always happens): Eva Longoria, one of my role models for beauty and optimism, was dying her own roots. I was shocked to find out that she had just as many greys as me... and a quick Google search confirmed that she was a couple of years younger than me. Crikey.

I wish I were as hot as she was!!

I couldn't wait for my hubby to come home that night and asked him, in the blunt European way that I do at times (as much as I try to be British, I can't always!): 'Do you think I should actually dye my hair again?? I know you don't find it unsexy, but still, what do you think??'

The look on his face: priceless. He looked like a squirrel in the middle of the road: shall I run, or shall I not, what the fuck do I do, help?? Poor man, he knew better: whatever he said, I'd have chewed his head off... so he sat there, thinking hard, and I mean hard, I could literally hear the sprockets clunking in his brain.

'Oh come on', I nudged in exasperation, 'This is not a trap! I just need to know. I find it hard to look at myself in the mirror now... I have no wrinkles or anything, but all this grey hair makes me feel uncomfortable. Makes me feel old. Or older than I feel... So I thought I'd ask what you thought. If you still find me sexy, I could probably keep growing it... just wondered??'

He took a moment – or two – before responding. He is the same as me, bless him, his big mouth getting him into trouble just as often as mine does, but somehow, magically, this particular time he was resisting telling me his real thoughts. Trust this man to be unpredictable!

'Just tell me what you bloody think, mate!' I nagged.

'Honestly... I think I'd prefer it if you dyed it again', he admitted, in the end. 'I'd always fancied you... If you choose to be grey, I'd be fine with that! But since you want to know what I really think... I like you hot. You are that hot girl that I fell in love with the moment I saw you. And I like you hot. Like that Latina actress from 'Desperate Housewives', what was her name? The one who is an ambassador for L'Oréal??'

Yeah, I know. He is in touch with his feminine side. I got him into that TV series a couple of years ago and we watched all seasons together. Could he not, with all the attractive chicks starring in the main roles!

Anyway, I gasped: 'Eva Longoria??'

He nodded. Then, after a pause, added, 'I like it that you make an effort to look good'.

That was, probably, one of the biggest compliments I'd ever heard from a man. In the past, he'd compared me with Sophia Lauren, too, on a few occasions.

He fancied his sweetheart: the girl used to being mocked for her looks. Who thought she'd die a virgin. Who was consistently told by her first husband her ass was too big and she wasn't tight enough after having had her babies. The woman who never liked her looks. Or her height. But did love her hair.

Yes, that is the one thing I do like. I may not like myself much, but really don't want to look old.

Reading what I just wrote, I know it makes me sound shallow and vain, but fuck that! This is my body... and my hair. And it is my choice to want to look good in it. Or as good as I can.

My hair is one thing I have control over – unlike my height. And I will keep making the most of it.

#

I'd forgotten just how smitten my husband was when we first met... I remind myself that my ex never in the fifteen years of our marriage paid me a compliment or said anything to make me feel good about myself. While this man does. And he does so every so often.

He fancies me. He genuinely wants me to be happy.

My hubby fell in love with me because he thought I was a hottie – and this is how he wants me to be.

Perhaps, after all, I haven't failed at love that badly?

Failure Seven. Music and the Little Girl

Once upon a time, there was a little girl. Her parents wanted to give her the best start in life. As parents do. They enrolled her in all kinds of classes in the hope she would find something she liked and would stick to it.

First, she did music theory. She was only little – kindergarten age. Her dad was a dedicated follower of classical music – a proud owner of a huge collection of vinyl records of all operas and symphonies known to manhood. In his youth, he sang in a professional choir and was, naturally, very keen on turning his daughter into a piano player. Or at least a choir singer. She was making good progress and one day her tutor recommended moving her onto the next stage – playing the piano. Then mum put her foot down: 'No way, this is far too noisy. We will be disturbing the neighbours and it will give me headaches. So, no!'

That was that.

Then she joined a school choir. Not through choice; she just had to. Anyone with a vaguely decent voice was automatically enrolled. She really liked singing, and did quite a good job at it, too, but was too tall and standing in the back row on the high platform on stage was ever so scary. She also hated towering over the rest of her classmates – as if she needed yet another reminder of how tall she was! And she didn't like the idea of having raw eggs to smooth her voice. Yuk. In those days, there was no such thing as salmonella or food poisoning. They were all as healthy as horses.

So, that was that!

Then she took swimming classes. Or, shall we say, a class. This is how long her new endeavour lasted. It was a cold winter season; her family didn't have a car and the swimming centre was not particularly close to their home. Whether she didn't dry her hair properly, or for whatever other reason, she got a nasty chest infection, so mum said, 'No, I don't you getting ill! Your health comes first!'

And... That was that.

Then she joined a drawing class. Wow, that lasted for months! She really enjoyed it (her pieces of art are still on display at her parents' place). Nice hobby it was – but nothing came out of it.

In the meantime, as it turned out she was very tall for her age, she had to take up team sports, which was the end of any other aspirations.

First, she played volleyball – didn't like that. Then handball. Really couldn't be bothered, but kept going to the training sessions, as she was a good girl. Eventually, basketball it was – for many years. As much as she hated running, jumping, anything to do with sports, she had to do it – to get people off her back and because it would have been a waste not to! After all, she was ever so tall! Even her dad abandoned his music dreams. He liked the idea of his daughter becoming a successful basketball star.

Years later... she didn't end up doing any of these so called hobbies. She took her own path. While searching for her way in life, she realised that music was one of her biggest passions. The only thing was, she could no longer even read notes. All her musical skills and knowledge were lost. She also realised that she loved writing. So she decided to write about music, which was the closest she could get to that passion of hers.

While being at uni, she started hanging out with local bands. This is when she found her real self. That was what she loved doing. Going to gigs, interviewing the bands and writing about them became her thing.

She thought she'd found the meaning of her life – until one day she moved to another country and got married. Then life became a daily struggle. Music and writing moved to the bottom of her priorities.

So, she grew up to be a big (serious) girl, with all due commitments for her age and marital status. Devoted to her responsibilities, she carried on with whatever life had in store for her – as was expected from a grown up girl. Music was always there in the background: in the car stereo, in her earphones at the gym, on the CD's playing in the kitchen while getting on with her chores.

This was all the presence music had in her life: reading about it, listening to it, loving it. A friend back in her home country, fellow rock fan, asked her once, almost drooling in anticipation: 'Now, tell me about all the concerts you've been to?' And wouldn't believe the answer she got: none. 'Seriously? You live in the Mecca of rock, and haven't been to any gigs?' Which is when it hit home. Yes, she was so bogged down in her small (busy, but still small) life, that she had not even thought of the possibility to actually enjoy herself and do what she did when she was young and single: listen to her music live, without ear plugs, letting it hit her stomach and flow with her blood stream.

... A few years down the line, there she was: at The Mecca of Rock. One of the biggest stadiums in the world; heart pounding with the roar of amplifiers digging into her stomach. This is what music was for. Yes, she was enjoying it. Very much. Still, something was missing. There

was no connection. As much as she loved the music she was there for, she did not engage with it. But never mind that; what mattered was that she was there!

Until one day it happened. She logged into her Twitter account (which she hadn't done for some time) – to find two follow requests. Her heart stopped. Her two most favourite singers wanted to follow her. Wow! She accepted the requests (fast, before they'd changed their mind!) and wondered, why would they want to follow her?? Next day she opened up her social media again, only to realise that one of these follows was fake: someone had hacked into the singer's account.

The other one, though, was real. No way!

The rest happened as in a dream. She had no idea what he'd been up to recently – as much as she loved his music (let's not forget how busy her small life was). Until she checked out his website: he was back with her favourite band, and they were coming to town touring in... two weeks' time.

That's when it hit her. This was the missing link. Connecting with her music was two weeks away. You can go to as many gigs you could afford or fancy going to, but still not feel it in your system. She knew this would not be the case this time. This was The Band. The one whose

CD's she had been stacking on her shelves for years. The one whose phases were longest in her life (she went through periods of continuously listening to the same band for days, weeks, sometimes months). With no hesitation she got herself a ticket.

The following two weeks were a blur. All she could listen to was The Band. In some strange, nearly surreal, anticipation. By that stage, she'd been to big bands' gigs before, but this was new to her. This was her band. Her music. This is what rocked her world. Even if only a handful of people turned up at the gig, to her this would still be The Gig of the Century. Because it was Them. And, they were back together with The Voice. Double the fantasy.

At the doors of the club it started to feel real. She decided to miss the support act and joined some other fans in hunt for food. One of them stopped just outside a pizza place and talked to two ordinary guys coming out of the restaurant. 'Hi guys, are you coming to the gig later?' Who the hell is he talking to?? She stared at them, suddenly realising it was Them. Two of The Band. As surreal as this felt, this was actually happening. In real life. The connection was made.

Two hours later it all came true. The Band was real. So was their music. And it was as perfect as it could possibly be. The circuit was closed. The Magic was there. And it was there to stay.

#

Reading this little story I made up about myself feels endearing. Yes, this is as much as I ever managed to achieve in anything remotely connected to music. Although, there is something I can actually give myself credit for, my work for that heavy metal website. Their editor congratulated me recently: apparently, I have published 100 reviews with them! Wow, how did that happen?

Perhaps the connection is still alive... Pulsing away under the pile of adult obligations and duties. Making my daily commute more bearable. And my long drives when delivering the kids to their dad. That silver lining to my boring existence.

This is what keeps me going. What makes my life a bit more complete.

I may be only a volunteer and not get a penny for my work, but it gives me such satisfaction! And I get all this music for free. Plus free tickets, should I wish them. Last year alone, I went to three gigs – all bands I absolutely loved! Paying myself would have been unaffordable for me, as I'd also need a hotel for the night. Plus fuel. Getting a journalist pass made it affordable. Also, having that special media access lanyard or wristband feels so good! Being allowed into the photo dip – best feeling ever!! At least for me. Not so much for those behind me: I tower over and block their view.

I don't actually get many requests to move: I think my height intimidates people and they feel a bit scared of me. But, anyway, I am always thoughtful and try not to obstruct their view if I can help it. I am good like that.

I didn't do concert reviews while I was in my previous marriage: why on earth would I want to go to yet another gig; I'd already been to one that year?? My current husband, in contrast, loves to see me happy, so, three gigs in a year it was! If there were more opportunities, he'd still have encouraged me to go. The sky's the limit.

He knows I'd grown up in a country where seeing my favourite bands was never an option. Not until recent years, anyway.

So, I never made it into music. I cannot play the simplest of instruments. I have lost the ability to sing properly, too. Being unable to read notes makes me feel useless.

Note to self: one day enrol in a music class, and learn to play something – no matter what. Just to scratch that itch.

Perhaps writing about music makes it less of a failure?

Probably not, as journalism was yet another nonstarter for me.

I had all the potential to be a journalist; in Bulgaria, of course, not in England. The pile of cut-outs from newspapers with my publications grew bigger. I got myself a qualification of some sort, too, alongside my degree. I had a proven track record of writing, so what was I waiting for?

All it took was a clash with reality. I got myself a freelance job at one of the local newspapers and was ever so proud of that. I was going to be a reporter! Until I realised that they weren't going to give me things to write about. It didn't work like that; who knew? It was up to me to go hunt for stories – and I had to produce one per day. Every bloody day! Where the fuck do I find those stories?? Ah, mate, you are on your own there, now go out and get us your daily publication!

I gave up before I even started. I got one story out and lost interest. I was not cut that way. I liked writing, but couldn't do it to order. Certainly not through fishing around in people's dirty laundry, or wherever I could find something worthy of editors' attention. So, I decided to stick to what I did best: doing it my way, and handing in my work as and when. No one minded, and I still got paid: happy days. The only one I disappointed, it turned out, was myself. They didn't expect I'd make it, anyway.

Journalists are like hunting dogs. They sniff a good story. They can sniff their own species, too, and I certainly didn't smell like I belonged to it. They'd immediately sussed me out, so no grudges were held and we still had good collaboration going.

No one told me I was a failure. I did.

#

'What else do you think you failed at?' asks Alison.

Well, pretty much everything I am good at. I may have many talents, but in none of them I am good enough.

None of my skills help in my career. If you could even call it that. In my job, rather. I am good at what I do, and it pays the bills. Not everyone gets to live the American dream. Or the British dream. Or any dreams. While some do, others just exist and make it through from payday to payday.

Will I ever be free to do what I want?

Interesting question. Not as interesting as another question, though: do I even know what I want? Do I want to be a writer? Journalist? Translator? Musician?

Perhaps. And what if I do? It is too late for all this. My life is a failure.

Rainbows

I have always had a thing about rainbows. Some people are obsessed with the beauty of clouds; others – with sunrises, or sunsets. I like all of that; nature gives me the sense of freedom and serenity; it helps me refocus and recharge my batteries, as cliché as this may sound. Most of all, though, it is rainbows that I am fascinated by. I have a whole Facebook album dedicated to them. There are hardly any 'likes' on it, though: people are, clearly, desperately bored of me posting pictures of yet another rainbow!

I remember my geography teacher from primary school speaking proudly of her daughter who made it as an artist: how fascinated the girl was with the clouds ever since she was little. I just shrugged my shoulders: each to their own. For me, clouds were plain boring, so the obvious conclusion was that I wasn't born to be an artist.

Funny enough, I remember a random conversation with my husband when I was telling him I find it frustrating that clouds (or gas, generally) look fluffy but you cannot touch them. He didn't understand what I meant, but asked: 'Don't you find it frustrating that you are very tall but not tall enough to reach them?' Now, that I found bizarre. Hey, each to their own, man, perhaps that was his own peeve hate: not being tall enough for something?

Anyway, back to rainbows. My love for them had another layer added in after I became friends with that uni band: their keyboardist, one of my dear short male friends, gave me some tapes to listen to. They, literally, changed my life. Another cliché, I know, I know! But this is when I discovered rock music, and we know just how important a discovery that was for me. From the moment I heard that first tape, I was hooked for life.

That tape was by a band called Rainbow, my first music love. It is still one of my favourite bands of all time. I wondered if perhaps this was why I was so fascinated with this particular nature phenomenon in the first place: as a premonition of something about to enter my life? There must have been a deeper meaning to all this, I thought, so, since then, started cracking the odd joke that my blood was type R – for Rainbow.

It was *that* significant to me.

#

A few months ago, I was walking along the same busy street in Oxford after work, on my way to the park and ride to collect my car. I had a vague feeling that this was going to be a very important day in my life.

Something was about to happen. I had seen 'signs' before and knew how important it was to look out for them.

The first time I noticed a sign was during an evening drive home. I had been, by then, chanting my mantras every so often: 'I am happy. I am strong. I attract abundance. Money comes to me easily. I am grateful for all the joy in my life'. And all that. The more confident I sounded, the more I tried to believe in what I was saying.

Needless to say, I was only chanting these mantras in my car. Or, obviously, as previously established, while on the toilet.

So, one evening I decided to talk out loud to my spirit guides. I don't remember why, but I was in one of those dark places, so I decided to call upon my angels and ask them for a sign. It was a cloudy evening. I randomly looked up from the steering wheel and, in awe, realised that the shape of the clouds surrounding the full moon was... angel wings!

A bit stupid of me to ask for signs while driving, right: all I needed was to have an accident! Not so clever of the angels either, to oblige at that particular moment, but they, clearly, decided to!

Since that evening, I started noticing the shape of the clouds and adding meaning to it. This was a fascinating discovery. I wondered if this was why that little girl obsessed with them, too? Children are, apparently, more connected with energy and the spirit world than most adults.

That morning, I saw a beautiful rainbow on my commute to work. At lunchtime, while scrolling through my Facebook feed, a post in one of the spiritual groups caught my attention: 'They say that rainbows are signs from angels. I asked my angels yesterday to give me a sign. This is a photo that my neighbour took of my house!!'

It was a picture of a house with an enormous rainbow over it. Fascinating, and, apparently, not photo shopped!

I never knew this about rainbows. This was, again, significant, I noticed to myself.

The radio I listen to in my car is a classic rock music station running a daily competition called 'Rock Legends'. Each day, they name a band. If you are the lucky one to get their phone call, all you need to do is say the name of the band, and you'd win. I'd been playing religiously for over a year, not missing a single day. Most days, I was entering for free online, but every so often I'd also do it via sms (which cost money) when the pay-out was higher.

That same day, the prize was the highest recorded to date. The band of the day was... you guessed it, Rainbow. I entered, eagerly, the maximum amount of free entries plus a couple of paid ones for a good measure, and my tummy fluttered with butterflies. Was that a sign? Was this the day I'd win the big money?

#

I have been trotting through life as a strong Amazon who always had her feet firmly on the ground. I never believed in miracles, or angels, or anything else extraordinary other than aliens. It was only after I convinced myself I was cursed (remember my Easter disasters?) that I started paying attention to such things. I'd say this was the beginning of what they call 'spiritual awakening' for me. I listened with fascination to an old school friend of mine, even more nonsense resistant than me, telling us all about a jinx someone had put on her, and how an old witch helped her lift it. Who knew!!

This is how I started discovering the power of energy, intuition and law of attraction. As I keep saying, I still don't seriously believe it all (which is why I never mentioned this to Alison), but I am getting there – slowly. This is also how I started practising Reiki: something I'd never think I'd get into, either. My life had taken an unexpected direction, and I somehow started making time in my impossibly busy daily routine for learning more and more. I started wearing chunky gemstone bracelets and walking with obsidian in my pockets.

In theory, I knew about signs already, I just never paid any attention to that stuff. I knew it from a book that made an impression on me in my uni years, 'The Alchemist', a beautiful fable preaching about how we all have our own life path and nothing can make us stray away from it; whatever happens, we'd always go back to our main path. Destiny, I guess. Things will happen along the way to point us in the right direction, 'coincidences'. Signs. Like the ones I had that day.

As I was nervously walking towards the car park, I checked my phone to make sure it wasn't muted: God forbid for me to miss *that* phone call! Then something caught my eye: a place called 'Rainbow and Spoon'. I felt as if a jolt had hit me. Could the signs be any clearer?? This was the day when I would win £150,000! The day that would solve my problems! At least the financial one, as it won't make me any shorter, obviously.

I will clear my credit card first, then put a few thousands to one side, and take the kids on a lavish holiday. A proper one, all inclusive, with entertainment and booze on tap. I will get us all new clothes and shoes which won't have to be on sale for a change. I may even buy a laptop for each one of us. I will also book whatever gigs I fancy. While walking, I started browsing the rock calendar for the rest of the year and drooled in anticipation. Not literally, you know. But nearly.

It will be the end of my daily struggle to clear my debt and keep on top of my finances!

Not that this is a life changing amount of money that would allow me to quit work or anything, but will help for sure!

I kept walking, smiling to my daydream, confident that this was the day I had been waiting for since I started playing that radio game. I knew that the time had come for my life to turn around. There must be a reason for all this spiritual stuff to come into my life: to help me get back on my feet. Everything happens for a reason, they say, and at the right time. This must be the time, as all the signs that day led to Rainbow.

I will no longer be a failure. Once I receive that extra bit of money, I will be in full control of my life. Psychologically, I am nearly there already, with a bit of help from Alison, admittedly. I just need that extra push! It will give me that self confidence boost, too, that I have been needing all my life.

Of course, money is only a fraction of my problems. But resolving it will help me keep my head up high and concentrate on the rest of my issues.

#

There was no phone call that day. Or the following day, weeks, month. The signs did not lead to anything. Nothing happened.

That extra help never came.

I was on my own. No one was going to solve the puzzle of my life for me.

#

I thought it was best not to share this little story with Alison. She doesn't need to know just how desperate I am at times for someone else to sort my own life out.

The Wild Swans

I am in the middle of chopping carrots for tonight's stew, when I hear a familiar song on the radio. One I haven't heard since, pretty much, the times when it was popular: my high school years. 'Rock Me Amadeus'!! I gasp, leave the knife to one side and turn the volume up.

Good job Nick is upstairs glued to his laptop; it makes him seriously uncomfortable to see me dancing. He only has two words for this, pronounced with a very specific horrified face: 'mum dance'. Apparently, it leaves him with scars for life.

I am turning the gas down, so the onions don't burn, and madly dance around the kitchen – as I do when no one is looking. I'd never heard this iconic song played on English radio. Tapping my YouTube app, I quickly find the official Falco's video and share it on my Facebook timeline. I am surprised just how many 'likes' it immediately gets: obviously, I am not the only one who remembers it. Just watching the costumes can make you shudder though: seriously?? But, then, looking at my prom dress, that wasn't much better, either! 80's fashion was a phenomenon in its own rights.

Next track on radio is even more iconic... and silly. 'Serious about the 80's', the host shouts out excitedly the station's punch line. They really are, aren't they! I cannot believe I am even listening to this... 'Karma Chameleon' is just *so* pathetic, yet I am singing along, dancing, and, again, sharing it on Facebook. I have, clearly, lost my marbles. So much for being a metal head!

I can't help but watch its ridiculous video... It reminds me of the glossy cover of the only Culture Club's vinyl record I ever listened to. As naive as I was in my youth, I didn't even suspect that Boy George was... well, a boy. That person was just so pretty and made up! His name wasn't on the record sleeve, so I had no idea who that was. Or they. All I knew was that this cheerful weird music had somehow managed to slip through the Iron Curtain – and that was as good as it could possibly get during communism: we were supposed to be grateful for any breadcrumbs we got from other nations' music dinners.

This was one of the few treasures I found in the enormous musical collection in the central library in my hometown. Jennifer Rush? I hardly ever heard her on radio, either... but her cassette tape left me mesmerised. 'The Power of Love' is still one of the eternal ballads I will always admire – as weird as that would sound to my friends who all know my taste for heavy rock.

This is how I slowly started getting to know Western music. Music we were not allowed to listen to which managed to trickle into Bulgaria through Deutsche Welle (secretly) and the Hungarian Cultural Centre (not secretly at all!), much to my delight. Music that makes me cringe nowadays... but was part of my overall cultural education.

In my childhood, that library was pretty much my second home. Or, come to think of it, the third one, as, strictly speaking, I spent more time at school than anywhere else. My dad was one of the permanent usual suspects here, too, and people didn't mind him. He was like a piece of the furniture. Didn't require help or anything. All he needed was for the library to be open and to be left alone.

Trouble is, he had *me* to look after during the many hours my mum wasn't at home. He finished work early, so would take me with him and leave me in the arts room, where he'd delve into the big glossy books (probably, immediately forgetting I was there), while I'd happily browse through the hundreds of vinyl records with fairy tales.

This was my heaven, too. I must have been young enough not to be able to read, but old enough to crave for literature – so, I'd put on those huge, comfortable, cushioned adult headphones and sit there for hours. I'd forget that dad was there, too. Most of the time, he wasn't, anyway:

he'd have vanished into some archives in search of something. The ladies who worked in that section of the library had pretty much adopted me at that point and, every so often, used to feed me more and more fairy tales to listen to. Or the odd chocolate wafer – as any good mum would do.

I only remember one of those stories. It gave me the creeps so much that I never ever plucked up the courage to actually read it. 'The Wild Swans'. Years later, leafing through an old and much loved book, I saw this title. It was, apparently, written by that same Danish author whose fairy tales would leave me in tears during my teenager years.

Hans Christian Andersen, together with Oscar Wilde, became a favourite author of fairy tales for me. I still sometimes read them now, sad and nostalgic. But never 'The Wild Swans'. I am still scared of them.

I have a book by Andersen that I sometimes read to my daughter at bedtime. She knows all about Ariel and the brave tin soldier, but has never heard of Elisa. She will never know why I avoid stinging nettles. Which is why she will never appreciate the biggest bravery of my cooking life: venturing into the nettles fields in the woods nearby to pick some and make it into soup. That took some balls!!

What dad did at the library all that time, I never knew. He was a bookworm – just like me. He lived amongst the endless shelves of books, making notes, while mumbling something to himself.

He used to make crosswords, so I always assumed he needed long or uncommon words to put into those little boxes. Now, I am not so sure: crosswords can't possibly require that much work; certainly not as much time as my dad spent at the library.

I wonder if this is how we satisfied some sort of fulfilment craving that he had. An internal need, perhaps not even vocalised to himself. This is who he was and no one needed an explanation from him.

Whatever it is that he did there, it made him happy. To him, that was the communist Bulgaria version of 'Cheers': where everybody knows your name. Where everyone smiled at him and wouldn't mind listening to his endless blabbing – in whisper, of course!

A few years ago a friend of mine diagnosed that: logorrhoea.

Maybe. But he did no harm to anyone and people accepted him for what he was. The library was full of others like him.

Freaks? Maybe – to the outside world. To each other, they were family. Which I was a happy member of, too.

To some, he may seem to be egocentric, or a weirdo. For me, this is the only man I would ever want as my dad.

He lived in his own reality. God forbid for him to argue with my mum! She wore the trousers in their marriage; there was no doubt about that. Still, he was dignified enough to make it look as if it was his idea to hand over all authority to his wife. I am sure they never had sex since my brother was conceived – what normal man would survive that? He did. And, most likely, this is just how he survived the lack of intimacy: by living in books and music.

Perhaps he did live in his own dream world. Or perhaps he lived in denial. Always thinking, deeply, of something. It could have been the next crossword, or his next move in the party of correspondence chess he was playing at that particular time.

This was actually a thing, correspondence chess. People used to play from all over the world, not through the internet of course, as that wasn't even invented then. They sent each other open postcards. All that was written on them was two letters. 'G8'. Or whatever. To him, that meant a lot. The postman delivering it was probably rolling his eyes in dismay: 'What the fuck? Why would you pay overseas postage for *this*??"

I will never know anything about my parents' love lives before they met each other. Non-existent, seems like. Surely, it wouldn't have been passion that brought them together, either: they didn't do passion. I am guessing it was the call of duty: their token of responsibility to reproduce and fulfil their civic duties to the world. Or something.

Perhaps this was his own way of dealing with his issues – which were, probably, not very different from mine! The issues of being a tall and intelligent man amongst midgets – in the physical, but also in metaphorical, sense. The team of engineers he was a part of was as sad as it could get. I never found anything to say to them, they were that boring and impossible. They were also short, with no exception. He stood out in the crowd, literally. In the huge dinner hall of their factory it was very easy to spot him: the only head above everyone else's. People called him 'The Long One': 'Hey, Long One, how you doing today?'

I never got to the bottom of this other dimension that dad lived in. He is still there now. This has also been his saviour since my mum died. His escape from the reality of his lonely old life.

Since I started work with Alison, it strikes me that I am, probably, not much different from him. Is this why I, too, have always lived in my own world, the one of books and music? Is it him I inherited that passion from?

I recently finished my counselling sessions, but cannot help thinking of Alison, wondering how she'd react to something I'd said or done, or to some random memories popping up in my head. She had become a fairly constant part of my life, so it will take some adjustment to keep finding my own feet without her help. A bit like a mum whose baby has just learned to walk unsupported...

She'd have been happy to hear about my dad. That could well have been the gold she was digging for!

Perhaps, instead of blaming my parents for most of the issues in my tall life, I should be grateful to them? Was it my dad who made me who I am?

#

My relationship with dad has always been a bit of a funny one. I was never really particularly close to him. Whenever we conversed, I'd easily get bored, as he'd talk to me about things that interested *him*. This is how he has always been: to have a conversation with him, one would have to be prepared to be talked at – instead of 'with'. I found that tiring. I wasn't interested in opera. Or symphonies. Or chess. Or the Second World War. Or most of what dad had to say to me.

Funny enough, for my Master's dissertation, I chose a topic that required me to dig deep into the WWII archives. I learned all about GULAG and Soviet concentration camps – which wasn't something dad knew about, but the knowledge I had, somehow, almost unwillingly, obtained from him, helped me cut some corners. I didn't need to learn as much as others would have to, because I already knew things I didn't think I did.

Thanks, dad.

As an adult who clearly likes rock music and has no music education, it turns out that I have more background knowledge of classical music than most of my friends.

Thanks, dad.

He spent most of his time at home in his office, doing whatever it was that he was doing. Strangely, though, I felt more comfortable confiding to him when I did something wrong. Those physics fiascos, I had no issue admitting them to him – while I had no guts to speak to my mother about my failures.

I always thought he was just large at heart and more lenient towards my errors... Which is why it came to me as a complete shock the way he reacted to the biggest mistake in my life: getting involved with a married man.

I know that our life experience makes us who we are and we learn (supposedly) from our errors. For that reason, if I were offered the chance to go back in time and change things, I probably wouldn't. With just one exception: this. When my parents found out, my dad stopped talking to me. He was silent for six long months.

Out of the pair of my parents, he was the one I hoped would understand and forgive me. He wasn't.

This is the biggest guilt I hold for my parents. This was their only great disappointment in me, after all those years of having the perfect daughter. The rebel in me, eventually, raised her head, and she chose to do it with something my parents would not understand: love, of the wrong kind for them, and lust, which they knew nothing about.

This is why I don't keep written records of my thoughts anymore. Until the day my mum found out about my relationship, I kept a diary – for many years. During my few trips to Russia, I had found some lovely notebooks with matte rubber covers, and brought back tonnes of them.

Month after month, they got filled up with my musings and experiences, and next to each other looked like the complete works of some classical author. What was in there were things that only some of my closest friends would know, or simply no one: my deepest secrets.

'You actually invited Ivan to that summer camp hoping to have sex with him???' she shouted in horror. The musings of a 20-year old virgin were not something mum would relate to.

I think I mentioned this already, but just for the record, I didn't sleep with that basketball player! This thought had been bugging me for years: if I'd agreed to do it, would he have stayed with me, and would my life have changed? Would sex have given me the self confidence that I was worthy of love, that men liked me, would I have chosen my lovers differently then?

One of life's 'what if's'...

The fact he broke up with me over this was not something mum would understand: I wasn't supposed to be having sex in the first place – not unless I was married to him. Which, it is fair to say, she would have happily approved of. He wasn't the cleverest amongst my friends, but his heart was in the right place, and he had a clear focus in life: making it into basketball. Ivan did achieve his dream, after all, and made it into a big team. For all I know, he might well have ended up in the NBA. And I could have been beside him! Two very tall people: the perfect couple. At least on the outside.

So yes, mom approved of him generally – as a platonic boyfriend. Not so much once she realised he was after getting into my pants – then she decided to totally dislike him.

Mum made me rip into small pieces all those notebooks. And it was a lot of them. I mean, like, shedloads.

Years of my life went in the bin. Years of my conscious efforts to hone my writing skills in the hope that, perhaps, one day I could use the thoughts documented on those pages to write a book.

Even then I dreamt of being a writer, a proper one.

How stupid of me: not to keep those diaries hidden! I should have known better... But, then, I never even thought of that – because my parents totally trusted me. They probably never did after that day.

#

I pick up the phone to call my dad. We haven't spoken for some time. I keep meaning to, and it somehow never works. There is just two hours difference between us, but it is surprising how hard it makes things.

When I decide to ring, it is typically during my lunch break – which is when the residents at his care home would be having their afternoon rest or quiet time, or after work – when they'd be having dinner. Bit of a non-starter.

This time, he is actually in the mood to have a chat, properly. My eyes well up listening to him. He hasn't been like that for ages. A year ago he had given up and was wishing his life away. Now the real he is back. Not much of what he says makes sense, and it is difficult to work out most of it, as his speech is muffled (we think he may have had a stroke at some point without knowing) – but he sounds cheerful and talkative. That logorrhoea is back, and, for a change, I welcome it warmly.

My husband walks into the room to tell me something and stops in his tracks. Noticing my tears, he gives me a hug. Once I finish my conversation, he says, simply: 'Book a flight, hun. Do it while you can! While he is still here. I will look after the kids'.

His parents have both crossed over to the other side, so the man knows what he is talking about.

#

My Messenger pings. It is that same Russian friend of mine, Olya: she has found some more old photos! One of them is of me and dad. I feel a deep pang. This is how I remember him, and how I had forgotten he looked, back in my school days! He was, actually, a very handsome man in his younger years! No wonder mum fancied him (or whatever).

Oh fuck. I miss my dad.

I miss those days in the library, listening to 'The Wild Swans'. I never realised how much he loved me – just wasn't able to show it. Now that he is old and vulnerable, he calls me 'dear' and 'sweetheart'. He never did before...

A couple of years ago I was saying goodbye to him before leaving for the airport. For the first time ever I gave him a real, deep, long hug. I didn't think he'd respond: this wasn't our thing, showing feelings.

I don't actually think I have been cuddled by either of my parents. Like, ever.

This time, he actually did. He clung on to me, tightly, in some kind of silent desperation.

This was the most meaningful, and sad, hug I have ever had. I prayed that this would not be the last time I'd see him. Luckily, it wasn't. But it felt like a final goodbye at the time.

Now I know I was saying farewell to that distant father who never showed affection or love.

This hug spoke volumes; it broke up the invisible wall we always kept between us that we weren't even aware of.

He is now a much warmer person. Funny how getting old affects people...

It was not his fault that both his kids turned out to be giants. He still loves us to bits, but doesn't know how to show it. We just never saw that.

What I did see during my childhood was another side to my dad. I asked for his help with homework only when I was absolutely desperate and had no possible way of doing it myself: usually in maths and physics. He would never just divulge the answer and would always make me work for it, hard. He'd take me back to previous material that I may not necessarily have had revised or understood and, instead, just brushed under the carpet. He was very good at discovering things I hadn't learnt and had no intention to. To me, that felt like torture, and I resented asking him for help. All I wanted was for him to do it for me – which was exactly what he never did.

Looking back at my childhood, I sit in shock, making a realisation that I now feel is important.

This is why I am who I am. He tried to make me an independent thinker. I didn't want that; I chose the easy path instead: going with the flow of the least resistance; doing what I was told; never disappointing. It seemed like the easier option then. As an adult who is now picking up the pieces, I realise that I have been, consistently, making the wrong life choices.

Trying to blend it, to go unnoticed, disguise my thoughts in order to be accepted, lie: is this how I should have lived my life?

I should have read 'The Wild Swans' and not run away from them in fear. It is only a fairy tale, and I couldn't even handle that.

Oh dad. I never knew what you wanted of me. I am so sorry.

Talent Number One: Cooking

'Oh wow! You are in the wrong job, girl, this looks so tempting!!'

I blush, hard. I am not used to receiving compliments – certainly not about my cooking! What I am used to, instead, is criticism: after all, I have been such a rubbish chef throughout the entire fifteen years of my marriage, I couldn't possibly be any good at it, could I?

'These chops are as hard as a shoe sole! And just how many times have you cooked the same thing in the past month??'

'These croissants should have been cooked at a lower temperature than this; then they wouldn't have burnt!'

'This Easter bread has been left to rise for far too long; the yeast has over brewed!'

'These cookies are far too hard, and you can smell the yeast!'

'At your age, my mother was already cooking a professionally stuffed chicken: emptying the bird, making her own stuffing and sewing it all up. You? You have never ever cooked a whole chicken, just the ready prepared ones from the shops!'

'Why do you always have to make the same appetizers? Your repertoire is so ridiculously limited, you have no imagination whatsoever!'

'What, you have been up for an hour, and there is no breakfast ready for me??'

All that – after I had been putting love and effort into everything I made, religiously jotting down recipes from my gourmet chef mother-in-law, spending hours on the phone to her in the hope to make a meal that could possibly compare to hers. Until one day it dawned on me: whatever I did, he'd always be comparing me to her. I would never be good enough.

It was a lost battle not really worth fighting.

Same as my old job: my boss would pick holes in what I did and criticise me endlessly, never praising any positive efforts that I made – which was a huge demotivator. I lost the will to perform and just plodded on, making one mistake after another. Same way I cooked one boring tasteless meal after another. Not enjoying neither the process, nor the result.

Interestingly, since I left my husband, the quality of my food improved. It actually shot up, somehow. As has the range of meals I'd come up with. And I started receiving a fair amount of compliments, particularly over the past year. Not just on Facebook, but 'in real life'. Friends coming over for dinner scoffing their food off; the kids licking their fingers and appreciatively mumbling with their mouths full: 'Umm... You cook this better than nana!'

Oh, do I! Now, this is the biggest compliment, ever: I cannot lie, she is the best chef I've ever known.

Their dad thinks I am a cooking failure. To them, I am the best cook on earth.

This most recent praise is written under my Facebook post with pictures of the mushroom soup I cooked over the weekend. The person who commented is one of my high school classmates. She turned out to be a proper chef, with her own cookery blog and everything. Praise from her is worth twice as much!

That soup wasn't even that fancy looking, really. But I did put love and effort into it.

I like posting photos of my meals every so often – when I feel I've done a good job. Not to satisfy my ego (which is not that big, as already established), but mostly to show my British friends what we cook back there in distant Bulgaria. Some of them engage and find it quite educational. Others are simply curious: now, this is an interesting idea, perhaps I should try this Bulgarian recipe one day!

I like to show them that there is more to food than jacket potatoes and Sunday roast. No disrespect or anything, but seeing my husband making himself beans on toast and happily devouring it... now that makes me cringe, properly: what kind of monstrosity is this?? Must have been invented by the laziest sod on earth!

I recall passing by a girl and a young man on my way to the gym in Oxford months ago. Obviously foreigners, like the majority of the city's population. They were, evidently, from those countries where people express their emotions without disguising them. No upper stiff lip: what they think is what they say.

'But come on, this is no food, no!! Beans on toast!!??' she exclaimed in an appalled humorous way, with all the appropriate gestures and display of disgust.

'I know, she needs proper food!' the boy acknowledged, matter-of-factly. The girl nodded, hotly, in appreciation of what he said, and they both went on talking about whatever it was they were talking about.

I don't know how I managed to suppress my laughter – although I am pretty sure they would have been fine with that: I was a like-minded soul.

Sometimes it is about convenience over quality – as I have come to realise during the long years of working full-time. So, beans on toast may be an abomination of manhood, but I quickly learned to give it to Nick when he was little. Kept him happy, and reasonably full.

It is easy to fall into the trap of fixing something quick and easy, and not make any efforts. After all, why would you need to, with the huge selection of food in the shops? It is faster and cheaper to use a readymade meal than cook from scratch. I know women who never cook. And that is OK. It works for them and their families, so, clearly, is no crime, is it. There is no need to judge others.

I never knew how to cook until I moved away from my parents to start an independent life in England. I was 28: an age by which most Bulgarian women would, naturally, be professionally cooking poultry, game, you name it, and not be failures in the kitchen like I was!

Well. I actually had a life while I was young... While I lived under my parents' wing, which was pretty much forever, I enjoyed eating out with my girlfriends, having a drink, going to rock clubs, reading my books.

Cooking just wasn't on the list of my priorities. Why would it be, I had my whole life to learn!

The first thing I was ever taught to make was pancakes. I didn't learn to make them until I was a student in England (so in my very late 20s)... but now everyone has pronounced me the Queen of Pancakes.

By everyone, I mean those I have cooked for since I moved away from my ex... As far he was concerned, my pancakes were, obviously, crap!

I could never cook properly... so how come whatever I put my hands on nowadays turns up undeniably and scrumptiously delicious? The photos on Facebook demonstrate the looks of what I cook, but it really tastes as good as the photos look!

Funny, that, I never thought I could possibly have a cooking talent. Perhaps I do?

I don't know. But it does feel as if a switch somehow flipped in me about a year ago. I hardly ever consult cookery books anymore, only when making something unfamiliar. Most of the time, I don't bother with recipes at all and just make them up as I go along, depending on what I have in the fridge and freezer.

I enjoy cooking now. And I don't mind if it takes long to make something I've set my mind on – as long as I have the time for it.

If only the worktops were a bit higher, though. All these hours of bending down chopping vegetables have got much to account for when it comes to my back issues. This kitchen has been made for midgets.

'Aww thanks hun', I respond to that Facebook comment, 'Glad you think so. It is one thing to cook for pleasure, though, and another one as a profession!'

Which is when I realise I have hit the nail on its head!

This is it: doing it for pleasure! Because I want to, and because no one puts me under pressure to perform. Yes, my husband adores my homemade meals from scratch, with freshly improvised recipes that I may not repeat again. His breathing changes when he is eating something that he really enjoys – and I hear this noise a lot when it is something I have cooked. But, then again, he is just as happy with soup out of a tin, so gourmet efforts are pretty much wasted on him.

It is the lack of expectation and pressure that must have transformed me into a good cook. Still, I have no chance to make this my profession. Not in a million years. But my kids enjoy it, and this is all that matters. One day they will be telling their own children that nana Vicky is the best cook in the world – and, frankly, this is as good as it gets! I need no credit for being a professional chef or anything.

I have another flash of memory. During the corona virus lockdown, that year when the population's mental health plummeted drastically, we had one of those fights where my husband decided to storm out and leave. I managed to reverse his decision, eventually, and we are still working on our marriage. What I remember, though, is how I dealt with my anxiety which was raising its head and opening its huge mouth, threatening to swallow me back into its black hole. That night I made my first ever successful beef Stroganoff. I'd only attempted that once, in my previous marriage, and it spectacularly felt flat on its face. This time it was an absolute masterpiece that Jamie Oliver would have been proud of!

This was my saviour in those times of duress. Planning each stage of the meal, not even knowing how I'd do it. Trusting my own intuition, not looking at Google suggestions, as I would otherwise. Keeping my mind on the meal. Chopping, stewing, stirring. It felt like a matter of life and death to get the meal right.

Cooking was the antidepressant for my escalating anxiety.

Together with a glass of wine. Or two. Not more than this. I have never ever been drunk in my life and take some pride in this.

Perhaps this is another reason why I performed so well as a cook nowadays: to survive mentally. This was just one of my many chores. Now, this is my safe place. Like books. Or music. And I don't need to make it a career. This is what I need, and I do not compete with anyone. It helps me be who I am.

A complicated meal takes my mind off things.

I only realise all this now. I may not be a Michelin star chef, but cooking has an important role in my life, and not being the best at it is OK. I still burn my pastries – but the kids still devour them. I still overdo the dough, or the sauce, or whatever. No one gives me grief about it, though. It gives us all a good reason to have a laugh.

This goes for everything else that I do. I don't have to be the best! Life is not a competition. It is my own story and I write it the best I can. I don't have to see everything through, and this is just fine! I can spend time learning something, and then change my mind. I am allowed to. This is my own journey and no one else has a say in what path I take – just me. If I stray from it, it is my choice whether and how to go back onto it.

I do not let anyone control my life anymore. I don't need their approval. I am good as I am.

I am not a disappointment.

<u>Success Number One: Reiki Business</u>

I stare at my phone, blankly.

'Hi Victoria, can I book a Reiki treatment with you please? I am around at the weekend if you can fit me in. Regards, Moira'.

This is a first! My Reiki business has been online for some time now, but no one has taken any notice of it. No wonder, really, as I don't have time or energy to put any effort (or money) into marketing and attracting clients. The holistic therapies market is overcrowded as it is, so it is only fair that the website I created gets no hits at all. Or, OK, a few hits. Per month! Yeah, I know. But, then, it is not like it costs me anything anyway: it is free, very basic, but free. And the money I paid for my level 2 course wasn't meant as an investment or anything. I just did it for myself, without any expectations to make money out of energy healing. I just knew I had to do it. In spiritual language, I guess I was drawn to it.

Perhaps this is one of the talents that Alison meant I had? I don't know, it is just something I was attracted to. I did it to help my headaches; in hope it would help me lift that curse and perhaps help me find my way in life. I did, frankly, pay a lot of money for it, money that I didn't have, but the teachers allowed me to do it in instalments, so the impact on my bank account wasn't too bad. It was meant to happen.

Anyway, no one was particularly interested in my Reiki business. Not until today, anyway. My Facebook page has not got any bookings, either. All that people do is sign up for free distant sessions: no one likes parting with their hard earned cash nowadays. At least not for treatments by someone like me who is, clearly, a new kid on the block, has no reviews or recommendations, nothing. So I don't blame them.

Then it dawns on me: of course, this is spam! I did receive an inquiry a few weeks ago and got ever so excited about it, so am not falling for it again. They do say for a reason that if anything looks too good to be true, then it probably is.

I study the email a bit more closely. The sender does come up with a proper gravatar, with a photo, phone number and everything. Her email doesn't look like a fabricated one, either. It is, actually, quite interesting: moira@moiraeden.com. Oh, she has her own website! I immediately Google it, and there she is, in all her glory: a proper Hollywood celebrity!

I stare at my phone, even more blankly now. This doesn't make sense. Why would a movie celebrity want *me* to treat her?? Surely, she must have a team of professionals who do it all for her?

'Maybe she is not such a celebrity?' a small voice in my head says, weakly. 'Or perhaps she just fancies a change? Or something!'

I spend the next couple of hours on Google, IMDB, rottentomatoes.com, clicking on all links with her name and reading everything I can possibly find, and it is quite a bit! Turns out, the sender of this email is genuine after all, and she is, believe it or not, based in the same area where I live. And she is a real celebrity, fancy that!

Come to think of it, our area is quite wealthy. Prince Charles lives not too far away, so... Hm.

Moira seems to be a director, producer, screenwriter, and even an actress! Not from major movies or anything, but the woman has surely done well for herself. Much better than me, anyway. Some of the movies she has worked in even I've heard of. A couple of them are amongst my favourites, actually. And she is about my age... which is a fairly depressing thought.

When I process documents at work, I never fail to notice my clients' age, and those who are younger than me get my admiration: they have clearly been more talented, or luckier, to get that much farther ahead of me in life. Although, in all fairness, some of this could be just pure luck, or being born in the right country, or in the right family, instead of third world (beg your pardon, communist) Bulgaria. Still, no excuse: a talent is a talent and will, eventually, shine through, against all odds. After all, even under communism people made it into the Wild Wild West, whether by escaping to the other side of the Iron Curtain, or just by being brilliant enough. And anyway, what is the point in comparing myself to others? I am who I am, and if there is anything I could have done to make my life better, I have clearly missed the boat, so better not cry over spilt milk or do self-pity!

One thing I have learnt from my newly started spiritual journey is to trust that everything happens for a reason. Perhaps my time will come, too?

If not – oh well.

Moira, on the other hand, is also editor-in-chief of a big art magazine. Seems to be single, travels a lot, to all sorts of glamorous and exotic places.

Now, isn't this what I would have wanted for myself: to live off my own writing that takes me all over the world…

Crikey, she was at the Oscars last week!

Oh wow.

My phone battery dies, so I put it to one side and contemplate in silence.

Could this be the biggest sign I have had from the spirit world, ever? I remember my rainbow fiasco and shudder. Hm, don't trust the signs, girl. It seems too good to be true.

Although, technically speaking, my psychic 'coincidences' have, by now, started to freak my hubby out, properly. Last week I made a point of noting each time something weird happened, and there were quite a few occasions, as a matter of fact. Walking down the street, I was complaining that I never get the chance to relax... and the second I pronounced this word, this huge pink sign on the shop window of a beauty salon jumped right into my face: 'RELAX'. Then, further down that same walk I wondered if the building of our local corner shop belonged to the actual man who ran it... and, sure enough, the second I asked that question, the curtain upstairs moved, and who was it to look out, if not that exact man! Spooky!

A number of small things like this keep happening, and anyone who knows about spiritual stuff will tell you: these are not coincidences, they are signs! Synchronicities, to be precise.

So, who knows, maybe this is meant to happen! My first paid customer is someone working in an industry I would have loved to write for but never could as a) I am a failure as a writer; b) English is not my native language, so I cannot possibly make it; c) I have no connections in the business; d) I have two young kids and a busy job, so have no time for any adventures.

A couple of years ago I got offered the actual position of a movie extra, come to think of it. I was to play some tall villain woman in a big movie from the Harry Potter franchise. Guess what, though: I couldn't do it because the days they wanted me on didn't fit with my work schedule. I am, simply, that pathetic!!

For all these reasons, I try hard not to get excited.

Still. Perhaps this is my chance to make it as a writer and journalist? She will like my services, we will get chatting, and I will casually mention that I am a writer, she will ask me to send her something I've done, and next thing you know: bam! I will be given a screenplay to write. Or she will help me publish that book (which I haven't finished, dammit).

Oh my God, oh my God, oh my God!!!

Fuck! What do I do now???

I text my hubby: 'Remember I told you once, it is all good that I am advertising my business, but what if someone actually contacts me for Reiki??'

His answer comes through immediately. For a change, I don't mind that he has nothing better to do with himself but sit on his phone all day! 'Yeah... so??'

'Someone has emailed me to ask for a treatment!!!'... To which all he said was: 'Oh?'

I type away: 'What do I do, what do I do now??'

His response takes a few seconds this time around. 'Panic!! lol'

Oh for fuck's sake. Very funny! Trust him to say something helpful. Duh.

So, this is exactly what I do. I panic. Properly.

#

It all went brilliantly. As if the Universe waved a magic wand and took care of everything. Without much hassle, either – which I found hard to believe.

The local spiritualist shop had a treatment room available exactly at the time I needed it for – in return for a small fee, obviously: it would have been too much to expect that the magic wand would also get it for me for free. Most importantly, Moira did turn up, contrary to my expectations! You wouldn't have guessed she was a celebrity: yoga trousers, simple trainers and a hoodie, long hair in a ponytail, big sunglasses, and the most charming warm smile. She didn't say anything about herself.

In the client consultation form, in the 'occupation' field she simply wrote: 'Editor and producer'. No big deal or anything!

'When was the last time you had Reiki?' I asked, making sure I sounded as nonchalant as I could muster. After all, I was supposed to be an experienced therapist, so I could compare myself to anyone delivering Reiki treatments.

'Oh, not for a few years!' she exclaimed. Phew.

'Ah, OK. Where was that?' I asked, intrigued. I was desperate to find out why she chose me instead of the other Reiki therapists in the area – and there were a few of us.

Moira didn't miss a beat: 'In India'.

Oh dear. No pressure, then! I suddenly felt hot and worried. Those butterflies in my tummy that used to visit me before each exam at uni – they came back, big time. I felt as if I had to sit one of the most important tests in my life. Job interviews? Nah, that's a piece of cake! Try pleasing a new, important client who has no idea just how inexperienced you are – now that's a proper challenge!

An hour later, I'd gained a new friend and dedicated client. Moira absolutely loved my session and committed to coming back again in the future. Happy days.

Naturally, I did not mention anything about being a failed writer and journalist.

But the important thing was, she had no idea she was my first client ever. As to how she found me, apparently, I was just there – whatever that meant! She found me online and liked my name. Wow, thanks, Daddy Google!

The weak voice in me spoke again: 'See, it was meant to happen! You have to trust the signs!' This time the voice was stronger and more confident. I remembered what my Reiki Master, Candice, had told me after one of our Reiki circles: 'You have to remember to put protection on yourself. Your energy is very strong, like a bright white beacon out there in the Universe! It will attract clients to you, but also negative energies, so you need to take care!'

Which also explained some of my headaches: apparently, I would easily pick up bad energies that got attached to me, so no medicines would help. This rang so true!

I emailed Candice once everything was over to share my news. It also struck me that Moira appeared out of nowhere literally the week after I'd paid off the last instalment of my course fees... Interesting coincidence. While I had been struggling with all those payments, month after month, not a single soul contacted me for Reiki. The second I cleared my debt – voila, a paid client turns up out of the blue!

Candice, as usual, didn't respond for a few days, by which time my excitement had died down a bit. This was probably just beginners' luck, something to add to my list of unsuccessful initiatives. Possibly one of my future failures.

Hi Vicky! Wow, you're doing really well with your Reiki! I'm so pleased that you're getting out there and practising it on people! Your confidence will just grow. With Reiki, it's really all about confidence, confidence to just let the energy flow. And no, I don't think it's a coincidence about the timing! Money is a Currency of Energy, so once you paid off what you owed us for the course, it would've been significant in Universe's terms. And also you're obviously ready as well! If you weren't ready, you wouldn't have attracted a client as yet. They get attracted to you when the Universe deems it is the right time! Best of luck, xxx.

I smile and let myself believe that everything will be alright. Everything is as it should be. Whatever is meant to be, will be. Or not. But there is no point in putting pressure on myself. I am protected by divinity – whether I believe it or not, is another matter. But Candice knows what she is talking about and this time I choose to trust her.

I may, after all, *be* a woman of many talents?

<u>Woman of Many Failures, Woman of Many Talents</u>

'Victoria. Can I have a word with you please?'

Oh shit. What have I done now?? Or haven't done.

I give Tom a pained look. He smiles – if you could say that. He never really smiles, but this is the closest it would get with his facial expressions: a particular tweak in the corner of his lips. Gosh, fancy being married to such a man!

'Nothing to worry about, nothing to worry about', he adds in some sort of an awkward rush. A bit unusual for him. He doesn't come across as someone you could make feel uncomfortable easily, to say the least.

We go to the meeting room. He shuts the door after turning the sign around to 'Do not disturb. Meeting in progress'. Right; this will, obviously, take some time.

Oh well. Another one of those conversations I have to grin and bear.

'How are you feeling?' he enquires.

I give him a long look, this one probably giving my head the shape of an enormous question mark. Just cut to the chase and tell me what I have done to get myself into trouble.

He clears his throat. Oh come on.

'I received a report from Occupational Health… Your counselling sessions have come to an end, I understand?'

Oh. So this is what it is about: a fit to work interview. He is simply doing his job. Got to tick the boxes and close my file.

I relax a bit. Perhaps I am not in trouble after all. I didn't think there was a reason for me to be: I have been doing my best at work recently. Or not just recently, anyway, but the bottom line is, I do try. As a matter of fact, I think I am doing much better in this job than in that old one in Essex. But you never suspect you have made a mistake until someone helpfully shoves it under your nose, and before you know it, you are deep into it.

'Well....' I shuffle in my seat. 'Yes, they have. We finished a couple of months ago, but I paid for a few extra sessions myself'.

'Oh?? You must have found it helpful then? Why did you pay, you should have said so? We could have covered the cost of a few more sessions possibly.'

I stare at him in disbelief. 'I didn't think that would have been an option, Tom... But yes, I found it helpful and I wanted to carry on, so I paid her. And yes, I feel better, thank you. As much as I can, you know, under the circumstances...'

He raises an eyebrow: 'What circumstances?'

I swallow and consider my next sentence. I cannot be ungrateful for what he has done for me, but there is a fine line between doing his job and actually caring for his employees. He didn't offer me free counselling out of the goodness of his heart, did he? That was a smart manager's move: to prevent more serious issues from happening by ticking the box that the company has done something to help my mental health.

We sit in awkward silence, until I speak again: 'Well, my commute and all. Nothing has really changed for me, Tom, so it is not easy. But Alison helped me pick myself up a bit and be more positive about things. Still it is a struggle at times, as my life is exactly the same as it was before we started counselling...'

'I see', he acknowledges. 'Well, we could have considered extending the number of sessions. It is not standard practice, but we take the wellbeing of our staff seriously, Victoria, and we try to help. You are a valued member of the team. Of the company.'

I shuffle in my seat again. This time more nervously. Did he just praise me??

I don't know what to say. Oh well, I could have saved myself a couple of hundred quid, shame but not the end of the world. What he has just said, though, is major. It sounds as if I may not be just a body in this company, but an actual individual??

He continues. Crikey, he has never spoken as long as this at any of our one-to-one meetings!

'We want to try and help you with what we can. If we were to offer you the option of working from home two days a week, would you be interested?'

Now my jaw is about to hit the floor. They what?? No one at my level is allowed to work from home! This is a privilege for managers only!

'That would be great...' I speak out in my smallest voice ever, after a long pause. 'I didn't think that was possible at my grade?'

Dear me, Tom is actually smiling! 'No, this isn't normally an option, you are right. But we recognise that your commute is more challenging than everyone else's and thought it might help you a bit if you didn't have to come to Oxford every day? During the pandemic you proved that you were able to do your job from home. You did a brilliant job, actually!'

I blush, hard. This is a first, for my boss to praise me!

'Um.... Thank you', I muster, eventually. I feel out of my place and, somehow, exactly at the right place. Somewhere where I am valued. This is news to me... and feels good. Nearly as good as I felt in my old job back in Bulgaria.

Oh hold your horses, Vick! The man is doing his job and doesn't really care much. All he is interested in is lower sickness records and high productivity. It is all about business.

'I like you, Victoria'.

I nearly fall off my chair.

'Yes, you are a hard working woman. You have integrity and you do your best. It must not be easy for you, you have stuff outside of work that stresses you out, but you don't let that interfere with your work. This cannot be easy. I know what it is like to commute, I did that for two years when I worked in Buckinghamshire, and wouldn't like to do that again. So I admire you for sticking it out and staying with us. I do. We care for you and appreciate you, so have decided to offer you a variation of contract and let you work from home for two days a week. It is not much, I know, but is something. The best we can do. At least for now. But we could revisit in a few months and see if we can do more?'

Is he kidding me, not much?? This is huge! No employer has gone an extra mile for me, ever! My eyes start welling up, so I look away and blink away like crazy to stop the tears.

'Oh Tom, this is so kind of you, thank you! I would love that!'

'Great!' he smiles with the biggest smile I have ever seen on his face. 'I will let HR know and we will send you your new contract in the next week or so. OK?'

I smile, flustered and still in disbelief. He asks if there is anything else I'd like to say, to which I just shake my head and smile though the tears which are just about to flood my eyes. Luckily, by that time his gaze has moved to his watch, then the door. He holds it open for me and pauses for a second before waiving me out: 'You do a good job for us, Victoria. We would hate to lose you!'

Now I must flee the room as a matter of urgency. I got into the toilet and let the tears out. For a first time in as long as I remember, I am crying happy tears.

I am appreciated.

#

I wake up with a heavy head and reach for my tablets: it feels like the kind of headache that won't go away without the help of medicines. My eyes feel sticky and my hair is damp. I must have been crying again. That would explain the pain in my head; tears are guaranteed to send me into a fully blown migraine at most times, so I have done well to get away with only a mild one.

I gather my thoughts and realise I have had another vivid dream. My mum was at the door of our old apartment in Bulgaria. I was just about to head off – not sure where to, but it was somewhere important. She hastily trotted out before me, stood outside the door frame and, energetically, poured water out of a glass onto the mosaic floor on the landing.

'Steady, now', I thought in amusement, as mum nearly made my trousers wet, which, surely, wouldn't have been the best scenario. Not just because I'd have to go back to change and would be late, but because I could not be possibly going back once I was on my way out: that would have been extremely bad luck, and mum was very particular about such things. If anything, she'd have made me stand there, fetch fresh clothes for me and make me change in the middle of the landing.

Imagine that, an innocent neighbour stepping out of their flat only to find me there, semi naked and flustered. Brr.

The water fled down the stairs, some droplets flying off to the walls and the balustrade, slowly trickling down, shining like tiny little diamonds. I beamed at mum in appreciation, gave her a hug and went off to whatever it was I was going to do.

This is an old Bulgarian good luck tradition. Mum followed it religiously. Before each exam, mine or my brother's (that was *a lot* of exams, which she somehow managed to keep an unmissable track of!), she'd be up with the crack of dawn, making sure we were up on time to a cup of hot coffee and a nice breakfast. There was no such thing as cereal and shit in those days. She'd have gone to the local bakery to get us buns, pastries, or whatever: all that fattening stuff I try not to eat nowadays but love, just love. When visiting Bulgaria, I cannot help it: the first thing I have to tuck into is those ridiculously cheap and tasty feta cheese filled pastries dripping with fat, and the marmalade buns with poppy seeds crust. Everything else can wait until I indulge in those calorie bombs, those edible memories from my happy childhood and youth.

This dream was, again, so real. Mum was fussing around, lively and happy. We were her life and she'd do anything for us, was the message I was getting through during the whole dream, and it stayed with me well after I'd woken up.

Most of all, she was alive.

My pillow was wet, too. I must have been crying for a while. Perhaps it was the sadness of missing her that overwhelmed me again? Or were those happy tears of relief that her funeral was a terrible dream and life was back to normal?

Nothing will be normal again. Like in a trance, I brew myself a strong cup of coffee and take a deep, heavy breath. I am going to do something that I have not done since she left us: pull *that* book out and open an envelope that has been carefully tucked away there all those years. My hands are shaking. Is it a good idea? I only read this once and it gave me a horrendous headache lasting for days. My magic pills didn't work then, as typically happens when the trigger is emotional distress.

I don't know why, but I have to read the letter again. This is one of those things I cannot resist the urge to do. Or maybe I can, but I know better now that I pay attention to divine signs: when I feel a pull to do something, I must oblige. Someone from 'upstairs' is trying to tell me something.

I know it is the right thing to do and there is a special reason for it.

I hold my breath, exhale sharply and open the letter.

Dear Vicky and Ivo

I hope your dad won't forget about this letter. I will give it to him with the request to keep it safe for you to read together when the time comes. I don't want you to feel angry at me for going without saying goodbye...

If you read this letter, I am gone. This is my goodbye to you, my dear children. I am sorry that I went without telling you I was ill. I don't want you to worry about me. You have your own lives and families to look after, the last thing you need is worry about me.

I don't know how long I have. The doctors said that patients with my type of cancer tend to live for no longer than five years, and no one knows when I got ill. I think it must have happened just after the two of you had left home, so I am guessing I have another year to live.

I hope you will not be angry with me. If I'd told you, you would have been making efforts to come home more often and spend time with me. This would have put you under more stress. You live too far away (Ivo, you in particular: I know it is not easy to travel from the States, honey), it is very expensive for you both and you have work commitments, so I'd hate to put this onto your shoulders. There isn't much you can do, anyway. Your dad helps me, he is such a dearing, bless him. I am taking all the pills they are prescribing me, so there is nothing you could do for me, I assure you. Please don't blame yourselves for anything.

I don't want you to feel sorry for me. I had a good life. I know you will be sad, and I know I cannot help that, but at least you won't have to watch me suffer, as my body starts giving up on me. I want you to remember me as the mother you always had: strong and optimistic.

Vicky, there is one more very important reason why I have decided to keep my illness a secret from you, darling, and I hope that you will understand, now that you are a mother. You are only a few months pregnant. Anything can happen during pregnancy, not just in the early stages. I have never told you that but I had a miscarriage before you. This made you even more special (Ivo, you are just as special, darling, but you will know what I mean in a second!). You know that I had to spend my whole pregnancy with you, Vicky, in bed, as there was a risk I'd lose you, too. I cannot let this happen to your baby, so I will keep my secret and pray that you understand. I know you will be such a brilliant mum! And I hope that one day I will see my grandchild from heaven. I never believed in this kind of stuff, and never prayed either, it wasn't what we were brought up with. But I do now. I will be there to watch over you two, and your children.

Yes, I had a happy life. I couldn't think of a better life, thanks to you two and your dad. I am so proud of the people you two became! I couldn't have been happier, so I am going to go with a clear conscience. I have always loved you so much. Perhaps I didn't show it at times, but I know deep in your heart you have always felt my love.

When you two left home, I lost the reason to live. Perhaps this is why cancer struck at this particular time. Now I live for your visits. Your phone calls and emails are keeping me going. I am at true awe at you both, how brave you were to leave everything you knew behind and start new lives in strange countries. You have always made me so proud, and now that you are grownups with your own lives, in faraway places, I cannot be more proud of you!

Vicky, honey, take good care of that baby of yours, and give him or her a big kiss from granny Vanya!

Please forgive me, kids. For everything. For being too harsh on you at times. For not always being there for you. For keeping the news of my imminent departure to myself. This is what a good mum should do. I know I haven't been the perfect mother to you, but I hope you will remember our good moments and let go of the not so good ones.

I love you and am proud of you!

Lots of love, mum

I have a flashback from another part of my dream. As mum waved me off goodbye, she quickly added: 'You will do amazing, Vicky, I am proud of you!'

I can't help it, my eyes are welling up fast.

She never told me in real life that she was proud of me!

She never called me, or my brother, 'honey' or 'darling'. Ever.

#

That day when my brother and I opened the letter for the first time, I didn't know what to expect. It was obvious by then that mum's life was slipping away (she was still in a coma), but what was it that she had to say? I remember trembling with anxiety to the point of actually physically shaking. I felt that was the moment of truth. What one says at their deathbed is pure revelation and remains with their loved ones for life. What would mum's last words be??

Would she say I was a disappointment to her, and how my brother had done much better in life than me? All my friends had acknowledged that he was my parents' favourite. As hard as this was to realise, I somehow accepted it and learned to live with it. He was, literally, a millionaire by then, while me, I was scrambling through month by month to make a living for myself and my family (by the time she died, Nick was four, so she'd done well making it beyond her expected death sentence).

My guilty consciousness was playing havoc. Was she going to remind me what a shock to her system it was to find out that her ideal daughter ended up having an affair with a married man? How I lived in sin with that boyfriend of mine in England? We did, eventually, get married, but it was a good few months before it happened, and I know that my parents will never live that shame down. They never warmed up to him... but this could have been for other reasons, which I didn't realise at the time.

I was such a disappointment to them, while my brother was the perfect son who made it big. He had it all, while I really didn't.

#

I put the letter to one side and have another sip of my coffee which has now gone cold. Somehow, a string of life events randomly pop into my head. You know how they say that your whole life spins off in your head before you die; it was a bit like that. I remember all the reasons why mum would have been disappointed in me. The failures and lows. I don't remember the achievements and the highs. All I thought my mother remembered were the moments when I'd let her down. Like those failure marks in physics: this is how she was with me, pretty much throughout all those years we lived together. Trying to get the best out of me, pushing me to achieve, while forgetting to praise me or just be kind in my times of achievement – because all I'd done was what she expected of me, so not worth a mention, really.

I remember how I felt after I read the letter that day. I was full of rage. I didn't want to feel that, but I just couldn't help it. She had kept her secret for years! My throat was tightening up with raw emotions... with anger. Why did she take away our chance to say goodbye, to spoil her in her last few years?? How dare she!!

I never thought she could actually have been proud of me. Funny how I didn't realise that when I read the letter originally. I must have been drowning too deeply in grief to have been able to get that. I wouldn't have been able to process it either, as I was not in a good place about myself. I lived with a man who on a daily basis was proving to me just how worthless I was, and I believed that. I didn't deserve praise because I was a woman of so many faults and failures.

I have come a long way since then. I no longer let people step all over me. Or mostly. I have changed. This is probably why now I find a whole new meaning in mum's letter, and it starts to melt me. It seems as if this letter was covered with a veil that has been lifted now – all those years after.

My body feels softer and weaker. I feel loved. Is this the love that came through the dream onto me, or is this the presence of mum in the room? I cannot shake off the impression that she is here with me, now, and is giving me a tight warm hug.

I have spent forty something years waiting for this hug...

I finish my cup of Turkish coffee and turn it upside down onto the saucer. Let's see what comes up, perhaps the reason I had to read this letter will become clear to me? Not that I have ever managed to do a coffee reading, but...

Well, this is a first. When I look at the bottom of the cup, there is, clearly, a heart there. Those tears that I have been swallowing now freely roll down my cheeks and I no longer try to stop them. Mum has drawn this on the cup, I know it.

She loved me. She really did. She just didn't know how to show it. Her parents never knew how to show their feelings, either, so she did the best she could.

And she was proud of me! I never knew!

I know why I had to read that letter exactly now: to remind me of what has been important all my life but I didn't see it. That I was very loved and appreciated, I just never knew it.

This could have made such a difference for me... If only I could have felt my parents' love and pride, I could have turned out a bit differently. A bit happier, a bit more confident, and possibly more successful. I could have chosen my men a bit more wisely instead of jumping at each rare opportunity out of desperation and lack of self-esteem. I could have seen the positives in my height and not let it define me the way it has. I could have been someone else, someone better. Someone happier.

Through the blur of my tears and emotions scattered all over the place, I see that it isn't my parents fault, after all. All they wanted was to raise me in the best way they could. They weren't perfect, but neither am I. And the reason my life turned out to be like this had nothing to do with the fact I was tall. This is how I interpreted it all, and I got it so wrong!

I cannot keep blaming other people for the troubles I have had in my life. It wasn't other people's fault at all, and certainly not mum's and dad's! They are the reason why I am who I am. They are proud of me. I should be proud of myself, too.

It wasn't the bullies' fault for not knowing how to react to my height. Haters will hate, idiots will speak crap. It was me all along, not accepting who I was from the beginning, and letting that affect me in such a negative way.

I am tall and this is part of who I am. I am beautiful the way I am. The way the Universe intended. Those who like that, or who take me as I am, are welcome in my life. The rest – I am not interested. They can just fuck off.

Yes, it is not about what happens to you, but about your response to it.

It is time I take responsibility for my life. For that fear I lived with for so many years and allowed to control me.

It wasn't my mother who tried to control me. Not my husband. Or my bosses. It was me all along: letting the fear get under my skin, deep into my bones and running into my blood.

I need to take responsibility for my own life. Now! Instead of blaming my parents for creating me, I feel grateful to them. I am the one who should write the book of my own life instead of letting others scribble all over it. It may not be a story of success, but is mine.

I am responsible for the Fear. And it is up to me: to break free of it, or carry on as I have been.

And make sure I teach my children the same lesson, and help them better than my parents managed to help me.

#

Oh, this is a bit naughty, I think to myself. No, seriously, I shouldn't do it! It is not OK to try and make friends with my Reiki clients for my own benefit. This is not right. The Universe won't like it!

I delete the signature from my email and hover over the 'Send' button.

'Oh come on', says the weak voice in my head. 'It is not as bad as you think! How will you ever get noticed if you don't put yourself forward?? A bit of self-promotion will not do you any harm! You are not doing anything wrong! You are not asking her point blank to do you a favour and put you in touch with Hollywood screenplay agents, are you! What you are doing is really quite subtle. There is nothing wrong with leaving your signature as it is!'

Well, technically, Moira has no way of knowing I have done all that research on her. Which is, really, called stalking, I remind myself. 'No, it's not! You have not hacked any accounts, or looked at any private information! You have just been nosy, everyone does it!'

The voice gets stronger, and, admittedly, a bit irritated.

I re-read the email I've drafted. It is really quite basic and as non-intrusive as it can get.

Hi Moira

I hope you are well? Just thought I'd drop you a quick email and check on you. How are you doing after our last session?

I add a few sentences about the visions she had during our session, and what they could have meant. I didn't know what the spiritual interpretation of water and rocks could be at the time of our session, so I'd promised I'd look into this for her.

Which is a nice thing I do for people. For everyone I treat, not just her: getting in touch to see how Reiki has affected them. Some get quite emotional, others feel tired, or overwhelmed, so it is important that they know this is all normal, and that I care. And that, ultimately, I don't just do it for the money, but for their greatest good. It is all part of the universal energy exchange. Or something. I still have stacks of books to go through to get my head around all this.

Moira, however, is different from my other clients – which have, indeed, started popping up every so often, just as Candice predicted. My first client is a celebrity, and I still have my secret hopes that she could be my avenue to success. The only problem is that she hasn't got the faintest idea yet. Yeah, aren't I modest, I know! Moira doesn't suspect anything about my writing aspirations. To her I am just an energy worker, and she likes coming to me for relaxing Reiki sessions. Like that tall lady I have my homeopathic remedies from. We became friendly, actually, because of sharing the same height (nearly, as she is about 190 cm), but other than that we kept it strictly business. What I am to my homeopath is what Moira is to me: a client. And that's it. How would she react if she knew I had a secret agenda?

Exactly.

For the first time since I have been working with Moira, I consider adding my full signature to my email. I feel like it opens another door towards who I am, and I don't always feel comfortable allowing people into 'that' world, the world of things I feel passionate about. Where I am not just Victoria Ilieva, but a Reiki practitioner, reviewer for a heavy metal website and aspiring author. Perhaps not in this particular order, but, still.

Not that I keep it a secret or anything, but there is something about my signature that makes me feel vulnerable, and I cannot put my finger on it. Depending on who it is that I email, I sometimes leave the links in, and other times delete them. Protection of my privacy or something.

I can't even believe I am having this discussion with myself over something so small. What is the worst that could happen? Lose Moira as a client? That would be seriously farfetched. This is just the demons in my head trying to get me to always keep a low profile. My ultimate goal to always try and fit in, and not to draw attention to myself. Being tall and not liking it has made me keep a low profile in life as a general principle. Which, I now realise, even extends to my hobbies! Wow, just how pathetic is that!

Yes, my height screwed up so much for me. Or, shall I say, I let it do that. I made a choice, which turned out to be wrong.

It is not too late to change this. Is this what I want from my life? To always blend in?

'How about that beacon of strong energy?' reminds me the small voice.

Exactly.

I remind myself why I volunteered to write those reviews in the first place. Because I enjoy them, obviously, but also with the idea of slowly putting together a portfolio of written work that one day could lead to something bigger. Who knows, I could get noticed by Metal Hammer and get asked to write for them? Or maybe I could gather some self-confidence and start my own blog; I do have a lot to say! Then I could get myself on the radar of some big lifestyle magazine. Being a columnist – how about that? 'A Tall Girl's Diaries' or something.

And why not? All those women writing their articles – are they better than me?

Well, yes, they are. For a start, they write in their native language. And they know more about their topics than I do.

Most of all, they believe in themselves! And do not try to fit in. This is the worst you can do if you want to get noticed.

Which is when the voice in my head starts giving up.

I remind myself of my sessions with Alison. I have come a long way to be who I am today. Self-deprecation has not been doing me many favours and got me into that deep black hole that I have been scrambling out of for years. Is that where I want to go back?

Or do I want to be someone?

That little voice now nearly shouts at me: 'For fuck's sake, woman, you *are* someone!'

I cannot shut that voice out anymore, it has blended with my own thoughts, and this feels right. This is exactly how it should be. It is a bit scary... but also exciting. As if I am *this* close to being free.

Weird. What is going on with me?!

'You don't know what is happening?' whispers that voice. 'You are coming out of your shell, that's what!'

I press 'Send'. With the signature on.

#

Dear Diary,

I am sorry I forgot about you during all these years. You know why this is, don't you? If it wasn't for you, my parents would never have found out about my first man, and I would have spared them all that pain. I know that I was living in a big lie, but it would have come to its end naturally, without breaking mum's and dad's hearts. He wasn't a good match for me, I knew it, so I would have broken up with him anyway, and no one would have known.

It is time to stop keeping secrets and living a lie. It is also time to stop blaming my height for everything that has gone wrong in my life. I have been making choices that have made me who I am today. And I have turned out OK. Today, I decide to take responsibility for my life and all my failures. And for all my successes!

I am a woman of talent. Which talent it is, I don't know. But, for now, what I do know is that I will write that book of my life, instead of only reading it and complaining the author did an awful job. I am a Writer.

This time around, I will write my diary without fear. I am an adult who can take responsibility for expressing her own thoughts and feelings.

#

The reply from Moira takes a few days:

Hi Victoria,

Thank you so much for checking in on me. Thank you, too, for doing further research on the rocks and water imagery. This all makes perfect sense! On Saturday evening I was completely exhausted, and yesterday felt very emotional, but today, I feel so much better. It was a great Reiki session, thank you so much!

I shall certainly contact you again when I feel it's time for another session.

Thanks again for checking in, Victoria. Have a great week!

See! It wasn't so hard, was it? And she obviously didn't mind that I revealed my 'true identity'. Ha ha. As if I am some sort of spy in disguise.

I shut my laptop with the feeling of satisfaction. This was close.

\#

Driving back from work, I do my best to not look at the sky: the clouds are fantastic today, and I am finding it hard to keep my eyes on the road. They say this is one of the ways the spirit world communicates with us: through the shapes of clouds, and I have a reason to believe this. After all, the first time I asked my spirit guide and guardian angel to send me a sign, they did exactly that: showing me those beautiful, unmistakable wings around the moon.

To be fair, the clouds have also played tricks on me. There was a point when I decided to apply for a job at another company, one closer to home. The day after the interview, when I was anxiously awaiting a response to my application, I came out in the morning to drive to work and saw this enormous arrow in the sky. It followed me all the way to Oxford. It couldn't be any more obvious! The clouds were shaped without any doubt to point West, which is where the new job was. I had to drive East for Oxford. I was convinced that the change of jobs was meant to happen.

I never heard back from that company. Not even a single line to say 'We are sorry but...'

Tonight, I park my car and gather my junk from the boot. Before entering the house, I stop. Something tells me I should look at the sky.

Right above me there is a gigantic cloud in the shape of an open book. Astonishing, breath-taking, amazing sign. The most obvious one ever.

#

After dinner, I casually scroll through my phone and delete any unwanted emails. Oh for crying out loud, the amount of promotional stuff coming through is just ridiculous! Note to self: unsubscribe from all these websites whose emails I keep deleting.

I stop scrolling. There is another email from Moira! Apparently, she sent it a couple of minutes after her reply yesterday, which is why I haven't seen it. Oh.

P.S. Just saw that you write also, Victoria. Fantastic!

Oops. She has noticed.

This time, there is a signature attached to her email, too! It contains the link to her own website and the magazine whose editor-in-chief she is.

Oh! So I am not the only one doing this! How interesting.

That evening, Moira and I exchange a few emails. She sounds friendly enough, so now that the cat is out the bag, I decide to be honest with her and show that I actually know who she is. I fail to mention, of course, the amount of hours I have spent reading up on her! But I do, casually, mention my writing efforts. Just as a friendly chat, and definitely not as in: please help me get into Hollywood!

There is something she said in her emails that sticks with me: 'It's fantastic that you write and also are a Reiki practitioner; both very creative pursuits!' I am not quite sure what the relation is between these two hobbies of mine, but who am I to doubt it, the woman clearly has more experience in creative arts than me, doesn't she!

That night I had a dream. In that dream, I heard a voice. It was mum's.

'It's time you write that book, Vicky'.

My mum, the one who made me rip out my diaries! Who never showed much appreciation for my publications: after all, they had nothing to do with my academic achievements, so she wasn't that interested. *She* is now asking me to write again!

Yes, that same mother who also wrote it her farewell letter that she was proud of me. She never said this kind of stuff to me in 'real life'. This is one of the major reasons that threw me into a deep conflict with myself, making me doubt that I was worth anything as a writer, and certainly taught me a lesson to keep my writing works as secret as possible.

For a second time, she came through in my dreams to say things she never did while she was with us.

Perhaps this is all a product of my own imagination? Wishful thinking? Or was it indeed mum's spirit coming back to me, to fix what was broken?

I woke up and knew. That cloud in the shape of a book and Moira's email came to me on the same day. This was a sign too big to ignore. I know that much!

I never thought I was creative, and never thought Reiki was creative either. Hearing it from someone else, from an artist, put the pieces of the puzzle together.

I am an artist! I *am* a writer! And it is time I put my pen to paper and finish that novel I started years ago!

I also know that this book is not going to be quite the same as what I intended when I first started it. It is no longer called 'Passport to Divorce'. It is 'Passport to Success'.

#

Not every journalist is a Pulitzer winner, and not all writers become worldwide famous authors. Which doesn't stop them from doing what they love.

Why did *I* stop? In the effort to keep myself out of trouble, to stay low and fit in. At any cost, mainly the cost of my self-worth.

I always desperately wanted to fit in: with my family, with my shorter friends, with the whole world. I spent my life making sure I didn't do anything extraordinary.

What if I am able to do something amazing? How do you know you will not succeed if you never try?

I am not a woman of many failures. Alison was right, I *am* a woman of many talents. It is not what you do with them that matters. It is trying. And even if nothing happens, that doesn't mean I have failed: it is just life taking its course. Whatever happens, is meant to, or not.

I may never know my purpose in life. But now, like 'The Hitchhiker's Guide to the Galaxy' goes, at least I know the answer to the big question, and it is: 'Write'. I, too, don't actually know what the big question is, but perhaps it will reveal itself to me what the time is right.

Or perhaps it won't. And that's OK.

#

I am leafing through the latest Cosmopolitan while I am on the loo – as I do. I see an interesting article about a lady who made it into

Facebook as their product design manager. Oh hello there, lucky lady! I'd have loved to land myself such a job, just am not clever enough for such things.

'You may not be clever enough for this, but are clever enough for other things! Stop putting yourself down, you are your worst enemy!'

Crikey, the small voice in my head has really... found its voice! Pun definitely intended.

Yes, I correct myself, we are all different and that is the beauty of this world.

I am sort of losing interest in the article and, instead, spend some time musing over other women's skills and career choices, and me. My eyes briefly scan the highlights of the article and stop at a question in a colourful box central to the page:

Best advice you've received?

'Standing out is inevitable, so it's best to just embrace who you are, rather than trying to blend into the background' – an amalgamation of the best advice I've been given over the years.

Oh! I nearly forget to wipe myself in the rush to pull up my knickers. This is huge, this is the discovery of my lifetime!

How is this fair?? People knew this all along, while for me it took me forty five years to understand it! All these years trying to blend in... while all I had to do was accept who I was and just be.

It really is that simple. As simple as a light hearted interview in good old Cosmo.

#

That evening I sleep with no dreams and wake up with a weird feeling. It feels like I am starting my life again. I am still the same person: that tall girl with the lowest of the low self-confidence. But I am also not that woman anymore.

I am a woman of many talents, and sky's the limit.

I will no longer put myself in a box. Who am I: a writer, journalist, or a business professional, or a Reiki therapist? Who the fuck cares! I am who I am, and I will take each day as it is. I will make the most of what I can. I don't live in a box.

Who knows, maybe I will be the next winner of the award for brave women who come out of their shells and take charge of their lives.

I grab my yoga mat and turn YouTube on. This is going to be a good day.

<u>Epilogue</u>

So, I am starting day One of my new life, and what better thing to kick it off than a 'tall' chat with my daughter. The equivalent of the weird conversation I remember having with my parents from my own childhood.

'Mum, did I tell you that a boy at school called me fat?? And that was some time ago, when my belly was much smaller than it is now!! I am a bit fat now but wasn't then!!'

Oh... Here you go, the exact opportunity to have that chat presents itself, isn't that spooky!

So I gather all my wits and positivity and give her a lecture. There will always be someone in life to find something wrong with her. Some may call her fat, others stupid, too skinny, too tall, wearing the wrong shoes, or not having a good hairstyle... And the list goes on. The important thing is that you are healthy and feel good in your body!

I finish my tirade, pretty proud of myself, actually, and beam at her, awaiting her response.

'Oh, I won't mind being called too tall!' she smiles, confidently.

A bit surprised, I offer: 'Is that because it is true?'

'No! Because I am too tall for a good reason!!'

Now I am properly confused and wonder what it is she has up her sleeve.

'Because I can reach things that others can't!!' she blurs out, proudly.

I silently gape at her and start composing my counter argument: yes but... And stop in my tracks. No, I am not going to correct her.

My little girl has got it right! She is not me.

My job here is done. I am only going to be supporting her in growing up as a confident tall girl, but she is half there already.

And this is all it is about.

Acknowledgements

Tim Ursaminor: for being the first reader and buyer of this book, and for his constructive critique

To the followers of my blog Not Another Tall Blog (notanothertallblog.com) for their ideas and contributions:

Denyse Toelkes

Christina Boone Scott

Gretchen Troiano

Sue Hendry Kite

Connie Adkins

Rodoshie Reheean

Gloria Goetz Miller

Jennifer Albolino Coopey

Alison Woodward